Latifa Zayyat was born in 1923 in Damietta, Egypt, and died in Cairo in 1996. She was educated in Egyptian schools and at Cairo University, obtaining her doctorate there in 1957. While still a student, she was elected one of the three general secretaries of the National Committee of Workers and Students which led the nationalist movement at the time. She was imprisoned twice for her political activities. Through her actions and writings she played a key role in the emancipation of women in Egypt with many academic, critical and creative works in English and Arabic to her name. At the time of her death she was Professor of English Literature at Ain Shams University. Her book of memoirs, *The Search: Personal Papers* was published by Quartet Books in 1996.

Sophie Bennett studied Arabic and Persian at London University and gained her doctorate in modern Arabic literature in 1993. She is currently doing research on modern Arabic literary criticism dividing her time between London and Cairo. Her translation work includes the novel *The Stone of Laughter* by Hoda Barakat and *The Search: Personal Papers* by Latifa Zayyat.

THE OWNER OF THE HOUSE
Latifa Zayyat
Translated from the Arabic by Sophie Bennett

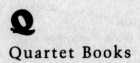
Quartet Books

First published in Great Britain by Quartet Books Limited in 1997
A member of the Namara Group
27 Goodge Street
London W1P 2LD

ISBN 0 7043 8043 9

A catalogue record for this book is available from the British
Library

Typeset in Great Britain by Intype London Ltd
Printed and bound in Great Britain by Caledonian International

Contents

My Experience of Writing

Writing, in the many senses of the word, has always been for me an act of freedom. It has always been one of the ways in which I can reinvent my self and my society even if, within the same framework, I have exercised the freedom which writing gives in many different ways.

My political writing, some of which was done in the context of my work as Head of the National Committee for the Defence of Culture, meant that I had to leave behind my hesitations. When I set it all down on paper and faced myself, I discovered my own position *vis-à-vis* events – and articulating that position gave it depth and definition. In my political writings, I also declared a position that was at odds with prevailing opinion. To adopt such a position required me to overcome my fears and go beyond the consequences, but the extent to which I was able to do so was the extent to which I was able to exercise my freedom. Every time I define my position and declare it, I find myself defined; my identity assumes its own features and I am free when I am able to imagine my existence taking concrete shape beyond the narrow limits of the self.

In my critical writing things were different because of the analytical method I used to adopt, although I no longer do. I would block out my subjectivity and, instead, subject myself totally to the logic of the literary work no matter how much it clashed with my own. I was liberated when, in my research on *The Image of Women in Arabic Short Stories and Novels* (Cairo, Dar al-Thaqafah al-Jadidah, 1987), I used other methods of textual analysis alongside that one, with the result that my voice appears side by side with the voice of the other, my logic side by side with his.

In any case, my work in the sphere of literary criticism has always given me a sense of freedom in that it has served as an affirmation of my self and of my abilities. It has been a means of contact and communication with the other, with others, and in that I have tried to transmit to others the pleasure that I find in the artistic work. The pleasure of making contact, of communication, has been an essential part of the freedom I exercise in all that I write, whatever its aim; I am only free when I make contact, when I communicate – and I find that same pleasure in teaching.

The freedom which goes with creativity is a unique pleasure. In every creative work that has issued from me, I was aware of my freedom as I wrote and, without being aware of it, as my concept of freedom assumed more solid shape through that work.

In *The Open Door* (1960: Cairo, second edition 1989, General Egyptian Book Organisation), the progress of the individual is linked to that of the nation in an organic way; together, the two form a plausible, comprehensible whole which follows a rising line from beginning to end, through the twists and turns of the plot; development is historical and social in this novel, at the level of the nation or of the individual.

The Open Door deals with the dialectical relationship between the freedom of the individual and that of his society – and the conditions necessary to bring about freedom at both levels. The novel suggests that the individual cannot truly find himself and, so, cannot find his freedom, unless he first loses himself in a whole that is larger and more important than he is – which, in the context of this novel, is the struggle to liberate the nation from the last traces of colonialism. The individual in *The Open Door* is relatively reconciled to his society; his freedom goes hand in hand with that of his nation and does not conflict with it.

The stories in the collection *Old Age and Other Stories* (Cairo, Al-Mustaqbal al-Arabi, 1986) show the self struggling against the self to achieve freedom. They show the struggle of true against false consciousness and the struggle of that which is won in freedom against that received through upbringing; the narrative engages with these questions on the fronts of values and behaviour. Man's battle for freedom is represented in this collection as a struggle that lasts all his life, as he throws off the shackles of his upbringing and education and keeps going beyond his class, beyond his society to what he is capable of himself. Individual freedom in the collection is never finite, nor final.

In the novella *The Man Who Knew Why He Stood Accused and Other Stories* (Cairo, Dār Shar-qiyyāt li-l-Nashr, 1994), an ordinary individual, who represents millions of people, stands stripped in front of a repressive social reality which snatches away the freedom of the indi-vidual by imprisoning him and which, by prying and spying on his house with sound and image, by forging and falsifying audiotapes, manages to convict him. All the way through, the novella raises a major question: can one – can anyone – enjoy even the least kind of freedom in an all-powerful police state, with the many means and mechanisms of subdual, tangible and intangible, which it has at its disposal? How far does the ordinary man – passive, preoccupied with his own life – question the gravity of this situation which extends over the whole in reality and not just over the few who are involved in political work?

I put an ordinary man, a man of no importance, in a position drawn from my experience when I was imprisoned during the 1981 campaign of arrests, when I discovered how my house and my brother Abdel Salaam's house had been bugged and how the recordings had been falsified, in order to gather the proof needed to convict both of us. That was of course a painful discovery, to say the very least – but every experience, no matter how painful, has a funny side. It was that element of comedy that I used when writing *The Man Who Knew Why He Stood Accused*, in an attempt to raise a mocking laugh from a painful situation and to make it possible to deal with the overwhelming, repressive reality.

In the face of such circumstances which held no prospect of any change, I was left only with bitter, mocking criticism – but even that was, at times, cheerful. For the first time, I found myself writing a novel that could be considered a parable or social satire. Once I was able to rise above my experience, look at it from outside, laugh at it and make others laugh too, I was able to take possession of my freedom with this scorn of mine.

The Search: Personal Papers (Cairo, Dār al-Hilāl, 1994; London, Quartet Books, 1996) is an autobiography, but not in the traditional sense; it is closer to a novel. *The Search* deals with freedom in various senses. In most cases, the question of freedom turns on two fundamental pivots: the relationship of the self to self and other, as well as the relationship of the subjective to the objective – that is, to oppressive reality. The question arises as the individual strives for freedom, sometimes hitting the mark and sometimes missing because he is weighed down by false values and behaviours or as a result of the shortcomings of a character who wavers between advance and retreat, between courage and fear, between taking the hard way and taking the easy way, between realities and fantasies about the self and others.

The problem of the freedom of the individual is considered from a very important angle in *Buying and Selling* (Cairo, General Egyptian Book Organisation, 1994). In this play, freedom depends not only on the nature of the social regime – the objective factor – but also on the individual, and the extent to which he is governed by the values of his society and overwhelmed by conflicts. Whenever he gives in to a desire that dominates and enslaves him, man loses his freedom totally; the desire for possession, for money and the power that goes with it, and the insane desire for satisfaction transforms some of the characters in the play into machines. Robbed of their will, they lose their freedom, their ability to endure and to rise up resplendent; they are prepared to sacrifice the very life of others at the altar of possession. Just as *Buying and Selling* shows the drive to possess money, it shows the drive to possess human beings which transforms people, the owner and the owned, into slaves.

This novel, *The Owner of the House*, brings out the many kinds of oppression – tangible and intangible – which bring people down, especially women, as a result of how they are brought up and what they learn from their upbringing, the process whereby people are brought into conformity with an oppressive society which refuses differences, demands sameness and insists on turning people into a herd of cattle that is submissive and easily led. *The Owner of the House* also brings out the difference between love and the desire to possess, treating the relationship between the sexes – based on losing oneself in the other or gaining mastery over the other – as one form of enslavement, in which equality and individuality are lost.

In *The Search*, I say at the age of fifty-eight, on my way to prison: 'I behold my freedom, entire and undiminished, at the end of the road.' That freedom was not finite, nor was it final. Now that I have grown old, I have to keep affirming my freedom time and again with one free and intentional action after another, whether taking action by the position I adopt or with words.

I lose my freedom every time I say to myself that the path has grown long and I should quieten down.

★   ★   ★

Between *The Open Door* in 1960 and *Old Age and Other Stories* in 1986, I have changed just as the world around me has changed, shaken by an earthquake that stops but briefly and then only to start changing things again.

In the middle of the eighties, as I was writing *Old Age and Other Stories*, I felt as if I were leaping blindfold into a sea. Because values and feelings have become more diverse, the circle of readers I addressed with my narrative had to be narrower and I had to know, without knowing in advance, what sort of melody the reader would respond to.

The economic, political and social changes that started in 1967 and are still going on today have meant that the vision of reality has become more complex. The paths to salvation are blocked to choking point. Values are no longer held in common as they were and different social strata hold different scales of values. The language of common feeling has been lost and people are divided among themselves; isolated, they have become islands, and lack the slightest sense of national unity or belonging.

As both my vision of reality and the social reality around me had become more complex, the style of *Old Age and Other Stories* had to be different from that of *The Open Door*. I had to begin, starting from the farthest point on the path of experimentation, to find new forms that would be able to gain purchase on the new reality.

★ ★ ★

The Open Door is a vast, organic, architectural structure that develops naturally according to the law of necessity through the struggle and its passing. It begins and ends at a significant point, and the ending delivers the reader to a new beginning, to an expansion in the depth of time and in the depth of history. Although before and after the July Revolution I stood to the left of the regime, protesting much and fighting much, reality as a whole seemed to me – despite all that was wrong with it – to be ordered, comprehensible, logical and justifiable. I used to enjoy the sort of outlook which is turned to the future, which sees history in motion and can go beyond the present moment, seeing salvation and the means to it in the future.

With *Old Age and Other Stories* I found such an organic form, carving its path with ease and certainty from beginning to middle to end, impossible – even though I perpetually longed for it and for the total vision of truth which is tied to it. With *Old Age and Other Stories*, questions no longer found answers, it was no longer possible to look beyond the narrow circle and so I had to use new techniques to express this new vision. I mixed a documentary style (diaries, memoirs) with narrative (a short story, a creative work) and intercut times and places. Many faces of truth appeared rather than one objective face, and the voice was caught between conflicting claims. Striving to go beyond became the nominal aim: going beyond the moment, and so did continuity – despite and in the face of everything – and so the style took on more than one level of meaning. In *The Search*, the organic form did not suit me as I wove the story of my life from the main struggle. As I mixed up times and literary genres and set them one against another, many images of the one truth appeared but none gave the lie to the others.

I would like to tell a story about *The Search: Personal Papers*. While I was in Qanater prison in 1981 and immediately after the search that took place in my wing of the prison, I wrote a short story entitled 'The Search' which appears at the end of the book and from which the book takes its main title.

The search in that story takes place at two levels: the concrete level at which the actual search is carried out by the prison administration, and the abstract level at which the narrator plunges into the depths of her past and evokes very different periods of her life that seemed, at first, isolated and contradictory. The external event – the concrete search – is, of course, what evokes the inner event. Through the perpetual interaction between the concrete and abstract levels of the search, the apparently contradictory and conflicting periods of the narrator's life are reconciled, set in order and brought together in a plausible, comprehensible whole, which, once the event is over, gives the narrator a sense of achievement and completion. She ends the story by saying: 'It crossed my mind, as I settled comfortably on the end of the bed, that I could now put my papers, that were all mixed up where they lay in their secret hiding place, in order.'

11

The papers of a lifetime really have been set in order. The ending of the story is of course important, in that it throws light on the narrative event and brings both external and internal aspects alike to completion. The use of the past tense 'lay' points to changes that have taken place between the beginning and the end, changes that have led to the papers of a lifetime being put in order when they had been in disarray. At the beginning of the story, the narrator mentions her inability to keep her papers in order. Something in the psychological experience she undergoes during the search, however, causes a change which enables her to set her papers in order, papers which come out into the open from their secret hiding places and can be arranged to form a plausible, comprehensible whole.

The struggle which the reader faces takes place at more than one level. It reaches crisis point and is resolved when the papers are put in order. They take on a symbolic value not just as personal papers, but as stages in a life that come together and can, finally, form a comprehensible whole. 'The Search' holds particular importance for me as it gets to grips with what in my own life has been a major struggle, and sets down how the passing of this struggle requires one to be reconciled with oneself.

After I came out of prison, I read 'The Search'

to Radwa Ashour and Aminah Rashid. Their reaction was encouraging, and Radwa said: 'Either finish it or publish it as it is.' Her passing remark struck a chord with me and I left the story for years without publishing it, gradually becoming convinced that it needed to be completed. It seemed more like an ending to a work, and lacked the background and the justification which would make its references significant. 'The Search' was about the main struggle in my own life and included the main events of my life, private and public; it also contained a solution for that struggle which, in real life, required me to confront my own self with all its shortcomings and also required a tremendous ability to go beyond and keep going, through facing up to myself this way.

In a subsequent conversation with Aminah, I told her that I had written a number of personal pieces on a number of occasions, on a number of subjects over a long period and she suggested that I might mix them up together. This seemed to me to be a fantastic and exciting suggestion which, although difficult, would not be impossible to accomplish. The suggestion took a deep hold on me, but it remained a suggestion and would remain so until I could find some kind of unity in the writings that were my personal papers, until I was able to put them together in an artistic form that would say more than a series of events and words could. My sense of artistic form in writing is acute, almost to the degree of insanity. I was aware that if I were to publish the material as a subjective work, it would not require unity nor would it require a setting for events. I was also aware that I could, if I wanted, publish my personal papers as they were, in chronological order. Such was my intellectual conviction, but my artistic inclination led me to favour meeting the conditions of the novel in a subjective work by identifying a significant, unifying event which contains the main struggle as it comes to crisis and passes, as happens in 'The Search.'

As I was re-reading some of my personal papers I noticed that the act of writing them contained, in itself, an artistic unity far beyond the unity of the character. I also observed that most of my personal papers followed the stylistic pattern of 'The Search'. That pattern was to link the particular to the general and make them interact, to slip from the external to the internal event, from the visible to the invisible world in a perpetual search which, although trying, took the self beyond its own shortcomings to reconciliation with its own truth.

Although my personal papers were very varied and although I had written them on very different occasions for very different purposes, I also observed that most of them directly or indirectly had to do with a major struggle in my life. I had been aware of that struggle while I was writing them, and I realized that it was the same one which is resolved in 'The Search'. This is the struggle between facing life head on and standing back from it, between expanding outward to embrace life and being turned in on the self, between advance and retreat, between making free, personal choices and seeking refuge in conformity with others.

Once I had seen this, the situation eased. The conditions of the novel were there, at an unconscious level in some of my papers, from the artistic unity of the event to the main struggle with its crisis and passing. All that remained to be done was for me to complete the main line of development by adding new material that had not been incorporated before; to reorganize the papers in a significant artistic form that said more than the sum of its parts; and to finish writing, revising my work here and there and transposing the unconscious elements that were present in the covert artistic form on to a conscious level. I did so.

I was committed, as far as possible, to the form of the novel, to a main struggle which passes following a series of complications and justifying factors which give momentum to the struggle in various different situations in life, including youth. This commitment constituted an element of the choices I made to include one thing and not another. I cut out all that was superfluous to the struggle and its justifications, and I included all that the struggle involved and which led to its reaching crisis point or passing. This applies to youth just as it applies to all the other stages of a life. My commitment to the form of the novel freed me from many of the requirements of a traditional autobiography. It freed me from the need for objectivity and proportion, from bringing in trivial details or aggrandizement. It freed me from the need to draw characters objectively, independent of the narrator's subjective vision, and from confessional tracts that may or may not interest the reader.

I enjoyed the freedom to include things or exclude them; I was in a position to choose what was significant and meaningful in a general context, rather than looking at the details of my life. While I did not conceal the events of my own life, I was able to consolidate my view of the general path of that life. I did not document it, as such, but was instead in a position to seek common ground with the reader, to identify the common elements of human suffering and sing the praises of man's ability to go beyond his situation.

Everything had changed. I still long to consolidate my vision of reality and, no less insistently, I still long to let the reader share this vision, convince him that it is right and attempt to influence him to adopt it. That is my aim in writing and, if I can achieve it, I cast off my isolation – or what I fancy is my difference and my individuality – and I belong again, I satisfy the insistent desire that I have had all my life to belong, utterly, in private and in public, inside and out.

This has always, always been the source of the desire which motivated me. I have never at any point experimented with technique for experimentation's sake. The techniques I have employed have been important or decisive only in so far as they have succeeded or failed to communicate my vision to others, and to join me to others.

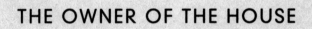

THE OWNER OF THE HOUSE

Chapter 1

The sound of the doorbell did not wake Samiya up but kept ringing in her ears, just as it had done every night since her husband, Mohamed, had been arrested. It was transformed, as it was every night, into a volley of knocks as she lay fast asleep, doubled up with her arms around her legs. Samiya straightened up and cried out as she realized that, this time, it was not a dream. She slipped into her houseclothes as the wind howled and the rain poured down outside: What do they want this time?

It took some time for Samiya to realize that it was Mohamed's friend Rafik at the door and not the police, as she had expected. She wondered what had happened to bring him to her door at that late hour. Since the day they had arrested Mohamed, Rafik had not shown his face. He had been supposed to come back while Mohamed was gone, although she was relieved that he had not done so. So what was it that brought him here at this hour? Samiya guessed that it must have something to do with Mohamed, although she was not sure quite what it might be. Had her dream finally come true? Had they let him go? She stepped back to make way for Rafik as he came in, whispering:

'I've been knocking fit to wake the dead!'

She regretted letting him in; he was aggressive and intrusive as always. She was astonished, as he barged in, to find that she had forgotten all about him since the night of Mohamed's arrest. His face had been wiped from her mind and yet here she was, acting as if he had never vanished into thin air. The thought made her angry and she turned to confront him:

'What do you want, sir, at this hour?' she asked.

Rafik warned her to keep her voice down. Why whisper? He tapped a cigarette against the golden cigarette box, keeping her waiting for a tense moment. Then he said:

'Mohamed is downstairs. He's in the car.'

Samiya rushed to the front door, pushing Rafik out of the way with uncharacteristic peevishness. Rafik stopped her halfway, stifling her cry of protest. He said:

'I knew right from the start you'd spoil everything. If Mohamed hadn't insisted, I wasn't going to bring you into this at all.'

Samiya no longer needed to ask why Mohamed was hiding in the car, why he did not come into his own house . . . one can never learn enough. Every time she thought she had learned something, she found out that what she thought she knew was an illusion. She refused stubbornly to learn, clinging to the last shreds of innocence. The idea she had clung to for an instant, despite all evidence to the contrary, that Mohamed had been released was proof that she had learned nothing. From now on, she had to learn to accept things as they were. If not, she really would lose everything. Rafik said:

'Pack your clothes and some clothes for Mohamed. Pack as little as you can.'

'Where are we going?'

'You'll find out later Hurry up, what are you waiting for? The police?'

Samiya took out a light bag and began to pack the clothes that she and Mohamed would need. Rafik, standing on the threshold of the bedroom, told her that the escape plan he had thought up was a devil of a plan, and when she asked him what kind of a plan it was, he ignored her. He emphasized that she had to follow his instructions to the letter, for security reasons and because he was personally responsible for her security as well as Mohamed's.

Samiya carried on packing in silence, wondering apprehensively where this journey was leading and how it would end. A night and day of tension lay ahead of her, of taut apprehension, of listening out for footsteps, of waiting – but at least not that sterile waiting, like waiting for Mohamed to be released. The police would not rest until they caught him again and, of course, the pursuit would be violent. Could she bear all that, after the year and more of torture that she had already been through? Rafik reassured her that Mohamed would be fine and that all would go well, Mohamed would deliver her safe and sound: she and Mohamed were ready to take Hell itself by storm.

When she came back from the bathroom dressed to leave the house, he told her to hurry. She dropped a toothbrush and some toothpaste into the bag ... that night a look from Mohamed had made her feel lost, and another look had brought her back. When the officer had wrenched Mohamed from her arms in the sitting room she had cried out – just once – and Mohamed had looked at her, his eyes full of criticism: You are not the woman I loved, his eyes said, and she felt lost. She dried her tears, pulled herself together and caught up with him on the stairs to give him a toothbrush and some toothpaste. The officer with the short yellow moustache said, scornfully:

'Do you think your husband's going on holiday or what?'

She turned from him with contempt, and Mohamed tenderly squeezed her hand. Her mother said the next morning: You're on your own, my girl, but she was not. Mohamed was with her in his absence. She smiled politely as she faced her family, which had descended *en masse* to take her back to the old house. Her mother said: Come back, but Samiya had pulled her hand firmly away — going back to the old house seemed somehow to be a betrayal of Mohamed. Her mother disapproved of the long road she had followed in order to go to university in Cairo and marry a man of her own choosing, independently of the family. On the telephone her mother said, over and over again: Come back. As the days went by, as Samiya waited in vain for Mohamed to be released, her mother's voice began to have the effect that it had lacked at first. Samiya stood up, picked up the bag and said:

'I'm ready.'

'Are you sure?' Rafik asked, a little scornfully, as he picked up the bag. Samiya took his scorn and shuddered inwardly as she wondered: What if he knew? What if Mohamed knew that sometimes, during all the time she had been alone, she had longed for the old house and its endless safety, for the monotony which nothing breaks and which the world outside hardly touches, for the silence which lies, still land quiet, over the old house, for the sound of footsteps which nobody hears passing, which cling to the walls as if they had not passed at all, for her grand-mother, with her white headscarf and white dress running her hand along the cracked back of the golden chair in the hope that the crack, which never mended, would mend, for the call to prayer from the minaret overlooking the house and the sound of her grandmother's dawn prayer spreading, in circles, over all Muslims, for the sound of chestnuts popping in the fire, for some place where one no longer needs to think, or make arrangements, or wait for anything ... Samiya sighed, annoyed with herself. She was alone and weak. If Mohamed had been with her, she would not have felt this nostalgia for the old house. But he was with her now, so she said calmly to Rafik:

'Let's go.'

The rain fell in torrents, covering everything with a thick fog.

Chapter 2

'Be prepared,' Rafik said as he sat down next to Samiya and turned over the engine. Samiya tied the soaking scarf over her wet hair more tightly around her head, and the windscreen wipers moved back and forth as the car slowly moved forward. Mohamed had not been there to meet her at all . . . when she had seen the black car parked some way from the house, she had flown to meet him, borne by the wind and, it had seemed, a lifetime of longing. Her whole being had melted when she had whispered his name: Mohamed, but there had been no answer. Rafik had gestured to her to remain silent and had swiftly and firmly pushed her into the front seat of the car. Slightly breathless, he turned over the engine and said:

'Be prepared.'

Samiya wondered if being prepared meant that she had to stay silent, not voice the longing she felt inside. Did it mean that she had to be prepared to endure being separated from her husband, knowing he was somewhere close by? Did it mean that she would not be able to meet him? Not knowing what it was that she had to be prepared for, she felt as if she would fall apart. Before her question had taken shape in words, Rafik gestured to her to stay silent, and the car slipped into the darkness as it pulled away from the house. When Samiya turned around to see where Mohamed was hiding, Rafik told her not to and, in a voice that came from the pit of his stomach, ordered Mohamed not to move. The car slowed down to a cat's crawl and pulled to a halt by the side of the road for, although he could not be certain, Rafik thought that the car approaching in the distance was a police car. It seemed madness to Samiya to wait for a police car on the main road and so, dismissing the possibility of making a run for it, she put her hand to Rafik's arm to beg him, in a whisper, to turn off into a side street, just in case, but the light from a street lamp was shining in his face and she did not ask. In the end, she decided that the car coming towards them was probably not a police car. She wondered, in astonishment, what Rafik was waiting for at that moment and she almost asked him but did not. He would not listen and, if he did, he would not understand. At the height of ecstasy, people do not listen or understand, at that moment which is the sum of all moments our whole being flows in one course, all that has passed and all that is coming. What kind of beauty is it that brings us to the moment of ecstasy, what brilliance? What meaning does our existence gain, the moment we ascend the highest peak to look down over the city as it lies at our feet, knowing it as we are known by it, pulsing with its life as it pulses with ours? What is this wonderful thing that Rafik, supple as a cat, is anticipating? The moment of danger? How could he possibly wait for it with such elation? Two eyes of light coming from the opposite direction shine and come back, shining brighter, blazing. Rafik leans over the steering wheel and whispers in a choked voice, as if to bring on the moment they will meet:

'The police.'

Samiya folded her arms, deliberately non-chalant. How could Rafik possibly welcome the moment of danger with such elation? He was relishing it as always, playing one of his childish games to show Mohamed that he was somehow better than she was. Samiya had enough time to work out what it all meant and, like a roll of thunder that threatens to turn into lightning but does not, the idea of betrayal gathered in her mind. As she slipped her hand from his arm, their eyes met and she realized now what he had meant when he had ordered her to be prepared. She would have liked to let him know that she was prepared, that there was no need for him to grip the back of her neck so hard. She heard a hoarse voice saying:

'Leave them alone, Farid, they're lovers.'

Farid replied cheerfully, his voice bubbling over with laughter:

'What a pity lovers aren't under our jurisdiction.'

The hoarse voice said, losing patience:

'Come on, Farid, if that son of a bitch gets out of town, she'll slip out of our hands too.'

Farid's voice burst out laughing as the man with the hoarse voice tried, unsuccessfully, to drag him from the front of the black car where he was standing.

'I'm not leaving until I get a look at her.'

The light from the torch took her by surprise. Unprepared, she found her head settling on the back of the seat as the light from the torch burned into her eyes and Rafik's hand, which had clung to her neck like a drowning man, died in a rivulet of sweat. Now she had to do something to keep the light from Mohamed where he hid in the back of the car, she had to turn the light from everything but her, tempt the laughing stranger to see nothing but her. How could someone who has spent her life fleeing from the gaze of strangers open the window to let strangers gaze in? How could someone whose flesh crawls at the thought of seduction be seductive? A voice inside her said: Smile, and her whole being cried out: I can't. A creature detached itself from her, a creature whose lips parted in a sickly-sweet smile. How could she? How did she dare? Where did she find the presence of mind and the ability to act, to behave that way at that moment? Did she grit her teeth as those two pairs of eyes stripped her, swept over her, as that creature's body writhed and coiled, alluringly, under the hail of obscenities and the smile grew more sticky, the cheap laughter more distant, the footsteps vanished into the depths of the night and the door of the police car slammed shut?

It occurred to Samiya as the police car pulled away that she had been through this all before, in every detail – but where, and when? She did not know, but she did know she had lived through it before and that she was split, a human being drained of everything and a monster with no roots and no power to move.

'Brave, she's a real *maestro*,' Rafik said and she wondered if she had become the monster they wanted her to be, a monster with no roots and no power to move? A lifetime of training had finally paid off, a lifetime spent hiding from other people's eyes and hearts, of isolation and deprivation, beating and intimidation, threats and promises, blame and punishment, of whispering in corners: Woe betide he who differs! A baby's swaddling clothes in two black eyes and a dead man's shroud, a look that quickens and a look that kills, a knock at the door, a cry that must certainly perish, woe if it is let out! Beyond the torch lies a bottomless pit. Woe to he who does not become a monster! Mother, father, grandmother, the minaret that overlooks our old house, my friends, all of you who cleared a space for me among you, here I am poised on the brink of belonging, as you wanted me to, I have come to you as a monster with no roots and no power to move.

'By the way, Mohamed, if I hadn't been behind Samiya we'd have been spending the night in the slammer,' Rafik said as the windscreen wipers started up again. Samiya leaned against the car seat and held back the desire to pour out what she wanted to say. It struck her that she had not felt afraid and, suddenly, she felt dizzy and sick. There was silence for a moment as another car drove behind them and, when it had overtaken them, Rafik took his hands off the steering wheel, which glistened with sweat, rubbed his hands together and said:

'Is that the way to do it or what? Honestly, my plan's really something else. Isn't it a brilliant plan, a hell of a plan?'

Samiya wondered if the gates of Hell would open and Mohamed would not reply. Rafik touched the steering wheel with his fingertips, turning off into a side street and almost – but not quite – hitting the kerb. Nothing was visible through the heavy veil of fog and the car missed the blind walls by a miracle. In a choked voice, Samiya cried out: 'Mohamed,' fearing again that he was not in the car at all. Not expecting any answer to her call, she started to mumble his name again. Rafik said:

'You can speak to her, Mohamed. There are no cars coming.'

As the raindrops fell, drop by drop, on the car window, Mohamed said:

'Hello, Samiya. It's good to have you here, sweetheart.'

Samiya closed her eyes and, without thinking, plucked at her dress, pulling it away from her as if she were afraid it might be dirty . . . she had not imagined that they would meet through that other one, the stranger. Mohamed continued:

'My heart is with you, Samiya, it's all been hot stuff since the start.'

Tears shone in her eyes. She relaxed and felt

the back of the car seat with her hand and then clenched her fist, resisting the desire to turn and look behind her ... she realized that she had to ask permission to look at her husband where he lay, hidden, in the back of the car. Rafik hummed:

'O, Attarin, lead me to some place I can buy patience ...'

Samiya shuddered. They must be in her house by now, they must have broken down the door, all the doors, scattered the books, the papers, the clothes, there were the dirty pans and plates she had left in the kitchen sink and onion peel on the table, her underwear that she had left in the bathroom and, in the cupboard ... if she had known, she would have covered it up but the moment had passed, she could no longer do anything about it, as she sat here, plunging into the heart of darkness, into the unknown, standing naked in the grip of their rough hands, in their foul mouths, in the blinking of their wicked eyes. Rafik said:

'By now they'll have sealed up your door with red wax.'

The sense that things were coming to an end settled in Samiya's mind. Stifling her anger, she asked:

'Where are we going?'

No answer came as the trees retreated, cast back behind them. The wind moaned, and the windscreen wipers moved back and forth. The moment of elation had passed and Rafik was like an empty sack behind the steering wheel, which glistened with the sweat that poured from his hands. His moment of glory had passed, it had soaked him all up and left him pouring sweat, the moment he had waited for and avoided all his life had passed. Was his life a series of disjointed moments? Was it her moment of glory too? The moment she had gathered all the weapons she had inherited and all the weapons she had learned how to use and faced the laughing man, on the brink of a bottomless pit? Was that moment, the moment she had saved Mohamed from certain danger, a moment of defeat, or one of victory? Would there be any answer as she plunged – who knows where – into the darkness? Had the journey just begun, or had it begun the moment she was born?

Chapter 3

The car headed for a small suburb of Cairo, went into it and, in a side street that was more like an alley, slowed down. Everything was dark, except for the light that shone from a small grocery store, whose owner sat on a doorstep smoking a hubble-bubble pipe. The car stopped in front of a large, metal-clad iron door.

Samiya stood by the back door of the car expecting Mohamed to get out, but he stayed hidden where he was. As she followed Rafik to the metal-clad door, she wondered if it had been agreed in advance that Mohamed would stay hidden. Was this part of Rafik's plan? If it was, then what was she doing here? The door opened without Rafik knocking, making enough noise to disrupt the calm of the entire street, but the street seemed to be plunged in a deep sleep. A man appeared on the doorstep and said:

'Hello.'

'The owner of the house,' Rafik said. She looked at the landlord in surprise. There was something strange about this man. This old man? Or was he young? His rich, deep voice did not fit with his short, frail body. Who and what did he remind her of? Had she met him before, not just once but many times? There was something strange about the whole place. The garden was not a garden to speak of, there were no flowers in it, just some land planted with lettuces and radishes and herbs, joining two poky buildings, one on the far right and the other on the far left . . . which one was she going to stay in with Mohamed? But how could she stay with him when the landlord did not know that he was there? Where was Rafik's plan leading? On top of the building on the far right, a tower with round openings caught Samiya's eye. She pulled her coat around her and wondered whether it was a dove tower or an observation tower and whether, behind those round openings, watchful, wakeful eyes were looking at her. The landlord said, shaking Rafik's hand:

'Hello, Mr Fayek.'

Rafik responded as if Fayek were his real name

. . . for security reasons? Samiya realized that the whole situation was false when the landlord said:

'Greetings to the bride. It's a pleasure to have you here.'

Samiya supposed that she was the bride and let the landlord know that his assumption was correct as he shook her hand, with obvious enthusiasm, and the watchful, wakeful eyes looked out at her from the round openings. Was this also for security reasons? With her hand in the landlord's, as he shook it violently, Rafik's plan began to take shape. Did he want to save Mohamed or stifle her breath? If he was the groom and she was the bride, what role was Mohamed to play? Or was there no role for him in this at all? The landlord was still shaking her hand, making her feel more and more awkward. Rafik nudged her, reminding her that she had to respond to the landlord's enthusiasm.

She began to move her arm up and down mechanically, holding the landlord's hand. Everyone who came into this house, apparently, must play a role, the role assigned him by the owner of the house. Did Mohamed have no role other than to crouch, freezing, in the car? How had it not occurred to her before that Mohamed might have frozen?

The landlord seemed extremely frail to Samiya as he slid home the iron bolt on the door and led the way to the house on the left, taking swift, sure steps over the mud path and the other one, covered with rushes. Rafik followed, and Samiya panted behind them. The landlord stopped, suddenly, pointing to the house with the tower on the right and Rafik struggled to keep his balance before he fell to the ground.

The landlord's face creased up with laughter and nudging Rafik in the ribs he said:

'Try another one, son.'

He and Rafik nudged one another in the ribs, laughing about something only the two of them understood. Rafik pointed to the house with the tower and said, with no trace of laughter in his voice:

'And you live here with your family, of course.'

'Alone, my son, cut off from the tree,' the landlord replied, and he and Rafik nudged one another in the ribs and laughed again. Samiya looked at the building on the left, which they were heading towards. It was tiny, like a doll's house. Could Rafik not have found a more welcoming place? How many rooms were there? Rafik had come to stay. Where would he stay? Where would she and Mohamed stay? It would be dreadful if they all had to stay in the same place, worse still ... Samiya pushed the idea from her as impossible, as she climbed the four stairs to the door. The landlord took a vast key-ring out of his pocket, big enough for all the keys in town; he chose the right key without hesitation, opened the wooden door and switched on the light triumphantly.

'Impossible,' Samiya said, as the trap closed around her. A single long room stretched out before her, like a corridor that one would expect to end in something but which did not ... standing on some broken tiles facing the door was a black iron bed, the bedposts almost disappearing in the low, grey ceiling. To the right of the door lay a bench, its metal insides spilling out on to the ground. To the left of that stood a cupboard with a cracked mirror in the middle and, next to the cupboard, a clock with a pendulum that swung back and forth. In the middle of the room, between the bench and the cupboard, was a dining table with four chairs around it. When she found that there was just one room, Samiya cried out:

'No!'

Had that other one always been there with her and Mohamed since before she set foot in this place, since the beginning of their relationship, she wondered? Almost accepting that the other was the inescapable fate of lovers, she would have liked to leave everything behind her and run away. But she did not have the luxury of being able to do so, when Mohamed was crouched, freezing, in the car. She ignored

Rafik's admonishing look and asked, not expecting any answer:

'Where are the other rooms?'

With stern finality, Rafik replied:

'The house is fine, Zahiya.'

The landlord seemed about to burst into tears. Rafik nudged him in the ribs and said:

'Don't mind her, the house is perfect.'

But this time, the landlord did not laugh. He stared at Samiya, seeming concerned. Suddenly, his face lit up and she dragged her forcibly into the kitchen. Samiya noticed as he did so that his body was taut like a young man's body, while his face was a mass of deep wrinkles. The light bulb is burnt out, he said, but the electricity is one hundred per cent and the kitchen is hygienic, it's the best one in town and the sun follows you wherever you stand to cook, by God's grace, some tasty little titbit. The landlord pulled her by the hand from corner to corner, here the sun, there the sun, while behind the window pane nothing showed in the dark but the drizzling rain and great, high walls topped with barbed wire. The landlord cried out:

'Sun!'

'Sun,' Samiya murmured, realizing that whoever crossed the threshold had to play the game of the man who owned the house. It struck her that she had always played that game and, although she did not know when and where, she was able to sense that the owner of the house had always been with her in one way or another, always and forever dictating the rules of his game to her. What, or who, did this man remind her of, she wondered? The one and only sovereign? Her father? The preacher at the mosque who threatened hell-fire and damnation? The teacher as he asked her to spread out her hands? Samiya withdrew, exhausted, from the kitchen and sat down on one of the chairs by the table. But the game had apparently not ended yet, and the landlord now tried to drag her into the bathroom.

'The bathroom's worth a look. I must show you the bathroom,' he said. Samiya pulled her hand away from his and said, apologetically:

'Later.'

Samiya knew from the look Rafik gave her that she would spoil everything, so she stood up to follow the landlord. In the bathroom, she did not manage to make the right response as he kept putting his hand to the light switch and then taking it away again, without touching it. Rafik saved the situation before it reached crisis point. Making the same movement as the land-lord, he said: It has blown, it hasn't blown, and jumped for joy when the bulb finally lit. The landlord rushed over to the tap, saying:

'Lovely! Mineral water!' and the game was on again. Rafik said: It does run, it doesn't run, and

Samiya hated the landlord, certain that Mohamed would suffocate in the car. Rafik blocked the bathroom door with his arm to prevent her from running outside. The landlord promised to fill the tank when the rain stopped, picked up the key-ring from the table and said:

'It's a lovely night, you two, and the night is young. Sleep well . . .'

Samiya stopped him before he left, and said:

'The key . . . the key for the flat.'

He hid the key-ring behind his back and almost wept, but Samiya did not waver and she repeated.

'The key.'

The landlord promised to bring the key the following day once he had oiled it properly. When she asked him for the key to the door on to the street, his face creased up completely and he seemed on the point of crying. Rafik stepped in.

'Zahiya, the street door hasn't got a key. It bolts from the inside,' he said. The landlord knocked on the door as he closed it behind him and said:

'All's well. I'm always on the lookout, and I don't sleep.'

Chapter 4

No sooner had she rushed blindly, recklessly out
of the flat, despite Rafik, then she realized the
folly of what she had done. The discussion she
had had with Rafik immediately after the landlord left had made her lose her equilibrium. She
was bitter as the sloe, he was calm and controlled;
for every question of hers he had an answer that
brought her back to face a reality she was trying,
in vain, to escape; Mohamed would freeze in
the car. Either he'll freeze or the police will
arrest all three of us, she said and he replied,
correctly, that her emotional flare-ups were
putting too much strain on their situation. The
fire is out, she answered, meaning also as far as

the landlord was concerned. Rafik told her that in their position, there was no place for emotions, they had to act like machines, to calculate and plan things. The fire is out, she said again and rushed, crazed, out of the flat to fetch Mohamed inside. What could someone caught between the eyes drilled in the top of the dove tower and the watchful, wakeful landlord possibly do? The dove tower, Rafik said, is just a dove tower, the landlord is just a landlord, and probably not as bad as other landlords and anything short of the Devil can be put up with, he assured her. Samiya sighed with relief once she had drawn back the bolt on the street door without making a sound. But she realized, as the eyes in the tower drilled into her back, that she had not calculated the next step: the creaking of the door would set the whole street on edge, so how was she to open it so that it did not creak? She had to be careful, extremely careful, for they were hanging on her every breath and waiting for her to go wrong. Who were they? The landlord, Rafik? How was it that she put Rafik, who had saved Mohamed, and the landlord, who was a threat to him, in the same breath? As she rushed from the flat, Rafik assured her that she would spoil everything. It seemed as if he wanted her to do just that. She felt confused as she pushed against the door a little then breathed out and, shaking, began to push again. She gave

46

the door one push . . . it was no use, no use being
careful, she had gone wrong and the landlord was
standing on the threshold, asking:

'Who's there? !'

It's all a game, that's the best way to describe
it, Rafik said, it doesn't matter if you want to or
if you can't, there isn't any choice in this world
of ours. Play, her mother said, and she repeated
it over and over again until the stone split,
detesting this game that was all worked out in
advance.

'It's me,' Samiya said. Sheltering from the rain
under a newspaper as he stepped forward, the
landlord asked, of course:

'Who are you?'

'I'm the bride,' she replied, losing her identity
and making a great step forward in mastering
the rules of the game. The game of the laughing
man with the torch was an exception, and this
game was the rule. But we're playing with our
necks, she said, and Rafik replied: This is pre-
cisely what forces us to play, as her mother forced
her to do things she did not want to do, clip-
ping her claws, taming her. She heard the
landlord ask, holding the soaking newspaper over
his head:

'Where are you going?'

Samiya felt certain she had been through this
same situation, with someone watching her triumphantly as she tried in vain to gather her

limbs together. Where and when? When my father was there in the old house? In the classroom, caught out by a difficult question? In the censure of a critic, in the careless glance under the shaming light of a torch? Her mother used to ask: Have all my efforts to bring you up properly been for nothing? She asked Rafik the same question: What if I were not prepared to play the game? What should I say now, when the only answer to the question is the truth and the truth should not be told? It's all a game. What should I do now, when not one word of the game comes to me? Samiya closed her eyes as the landlord nudged her in the ribs and asked:

'Are you going to get a beer?'

She did not understand what he was saying. When he asked her again, he threw her a lifeline without knowing it as the door of the grocery shop nearby was open. Judging it necessary to stay silent, she begrudged him an answer as his question was out of any context. He winked at her suggestively and said:

'Tonight a beer would be nice . . . the night is young.'

'We want bread, just some bread,' Samiya said. The landlord's eyes shone like pearls and the look in them said: Not me, girl, play another one. He stopped laughing and signalled to Samiya to come close to him. He said in a conspiratorial tone:

'Shall I come with you?'

Samiya shook her head, and the landlord stamped his foot on the ground, spattering them both with mud and, when he said:

'I must come with you,' she would have liked to grab him by the throat. Play, Samiya, play, all your life you have had to play so what's stopping you now? Your mother's words echo in your ears, splitting the stone, your husband is freezing in the car and you have to play, there is no choice. Gather together the words of the game, all you have inherited and all that you have learned, and play. Samiya set the hair ribbon straight in her hair and said, in a honeyed voice as if she were speaking to a child:

'What? ! Us go out and leave the house all on its own like that?'

'I'll wait for you to come back, and close the door after you,' the landlord said and he rushed off to the house. Samiya slipped out . . . she had to act quickly, before the landlord realized: she had to get Mohamed in safely, quietly, just get him out of the circle of light that was catching up with him. How? Mohamed is not there, Rafik said, do you remember . . . a pair of newly-weds, simple but smart. If the landlord finds out that Mohamed is here, it will be a harsh blow. There's no doubt about that. How long would they remain at the landlord's mercy, she wondered? Rafik said: God in His wisdom knows best, imitating an old woman's voice. Samiya rushed over to the car, looking around her. She stood facing away from the house and pulled the rear door handle, whispering:

'Mohamed.'

'You took your time, Samiya,' he said as Samiya threw him her headscarf and took off her coat.

'Put these on.'

Mohamed sat on the floor of the car and turned his back on her, facing the house, as she helped him into her coat.

'Straight ahead, the house on the left,' she whispered. As he got out of the car, Mohamed asked:

'What about you?'

'I'll come in right after you . . . go on!' Pointing in the headscarf and her overcoat she said apologetically:

'Sorry, it's the only way.'

Mohamed did not hear the end of her sentence. He bent down, went around the car and dashed through the door. Samiya held her breath as she watched him move forward. She would follow him inside as soon as he was out of the circle of light. She let out her breath all at once, turning the air to smoke. She went up to the door on the street, imagining Rafik's face when she went in to him smiling triumphantly. But suddenly, she froze where she stood by the door

. . . from inside, the landlord's voice came to her saying to her husband, to her:

'Sleep well . . . congratulations, and I hope it all goes well.'

The door closed on Samiya and she let go of it without noticing, as the bolt creaked home on the inside and a rich, deep voice broken by coughing said over and over again, in a singsong tone:

'All is well, all is well.'

Chapter 5

Samiya stood hunched by the door, pulling her
dress down over her legs to protect them from
the stinging wind and rain. She could take shelter
in the car, but it would be better for her to stay
close by the door so that she could slip inside as
soon as it opened. She brushed her hair from
her neck with her hand, wringing the water
from it . . . she had to keep a grip on herself.
She would not have to wait long. Mohamed
would open the door, no matter what it cost
him. Of that fact there was no doubt . . . I want
to do something for you, Mohamed said, his lips
brushing over her lowered eyelids as the wind
bore the overwhelmingly intense fragrance of

jasmine to her from the neighbouring gardens and the tears shone in her eyes. Enough?! He laughed, filling her hands with apricot blossom. I want a whole tree. No, that would be some story, wouldn't it, a tree needs a garden and a garden needs a house and a house needs . . . and she covered his mouth with her hand to stop him from going on, not wanting to let him spoil the dream she was living by speaking of material things. When Mohamed's arm was around her waist, the dream seemed a reality to them both.

Samiya ran to the door, holding her breath as she strained to hear the footsteps that did not come . . . in her bed, she had strained to hear those voices that did not come. What if they had come? Voices on the point of taking shape in words that do not take shape, as she lies motionless on the bed, her eyes bright, when would the call come? She did not know, but she felt it in every cell of her body and the air was so heavy with it that she imagined she could put out her hand and take hold of it, the call would come – perhaps tomorrow, perhaps today, now, and then she would know perfect happiness, she would hold on to it and never let it go, would not let it slip away. Happiness was her right and her destiny, all she had to do was put out her hand and take hold of it and the whole world would lie at her feet . . . I am young and beautiful, in every cell of my body are oceans of tenderness that no one has known, my lips are an opening fig moist with dew on which the dawn has not yet risen. My cheeks are flushed with the wine of life, my eyes are a lake of honey that reflects only beauty, so when will the call come? Voices on the point of becoming clear that do not become clear, on the point of forming that do not form . . .

With a sense of defeat, Samiya stepped back from the door. What she had heard was not footsteps creeping to the door but the rustling of leaves. Light. Did she see a glimmer of light? She looked through the keyhole in the iron door . . . there was light, for sure, slipping out from the threshold of a door. Mohamed must be on his way to her. She would not have to wait for long. We aren't on a honeymoon or some pleasure cruise, Rafik said, when she was upset that he had not found a better or more welcoming place, a place with some privacy for her and Mohamed. Rafik told her that things were relative, and the time factor and the danger factor had governed the choice. She wondered if she was slow to understand or if she was rejecting reality and escaping to a world that existed only in her imagination, some world that was not the real world?

Yes, everyone who comes into this house has to put on a disguise, he said, and that's enough talk of absolutes and identity and all that nonsense. Yes, we have to adapt to our circumstances, things are relative, the fittest survive and false names saved Mohamed from prison. Who am I? Who am I, she kept repeating, salvation a hair's breadth from perdition as the laughing man shines his torch in your eyes.

Finally, in the end she would get to bed, get somewhere warm, she thought, as she heard footsteps approaching. Was it Mohamed or Rafik? These feet are striding, not creeping. Terror paralyses her, these feet strike the ground firmly as if they owned the earth and everything on it. Samiya hid behind a tree and clung to it wishing it would open up and swallow her, as a soldier passed by on his patrol . . . he would come back, he would come back for sure. She stole over to the locked iron door, feeling it with her hand as if it might open up to her and let her in . . . don't close the door on me, my love, I beg of you, do not close the door, let me in. Every cell of my body is filled with love past and future, folds upon folds of love that I wove every night in my bed while I was waiting for you . . . my bed is cold without you, a tomb that holds me without the sleep of death, a tomb filled with the wakefulness of deprivation, with troubled dreams, with the loneliness of death . . . when will my isolation be broken? You turned from me, your shoulder pressed to mine, your fragrance in my nose, in my body, my fingertips. Is it your fragrance, or mine, or our fragrance? Is it not you or I but that unique person that is us . . . at that moment, I longed for death.

I should like to ask you now, why did I long for death then as I rose to the peak beyond which there is no peak, as warmth spread out to us from the stove and the glow of the fire was reflected in your face. I relax, warming my hands by the fire and waiting for you to reply. In an instant you will speak, in a moment we will become that unique person that is us, in a moment I will know all that I ever longed to know, understand all that I was never able to understand, in a moment I will set out with you for the peak beyond which there is no peak . . . why do you not say anything, my love, why do you not speak? There is no time. There is no time to relax, to talk. No time to meet with someone else and even if it does happen it does not last, nothing lasts, one has to turn away from the peak to the foothills . . . why do you not open the door to me, my love? Why do you not speak? Perhaps you opened the door without my seeing, spoke without my hearing . . . my eyes are open, watching and I saw nothing, my ears are listening and I heard nothing . . . what can have distracted me from you? A knock at the door, the light of a torch burning my eyes, the eyes from the tower drilling into my back, the regular footsteps that were born the day I was born, was this all I could see and hear, the sound of those feet that strike the ground firmly as if they owned the earth and everything on it?

Samiya was filled with an overwhelming desire to throw herself into the middle of the road so that the footsteps would crush her. As they drew close again, she no longer saw or heard anything. She did not move from where she stood, did not slip behind the tree to hide as she should have done and did not throw herself into the road as she wanted to. She stood trembling by the door, by the glimmer of light. The patrol soldier passed by, half asleep, and did not see her.

When he had vanished back where he came from, Samiya began to search for a crack in the wall around the house. She felt the wall carefully from top to bottom, reaching up as high as she could and twisting down until she was almost on her knees . . . there must be a crack in it somewhere that she could use to get inside . . . it was not within her reach, as she had imagined when she was sixteen. Her hand touched nothing but stone as she slowly moved along the wall, stretching and twisting, one step at a time. A fine thread of blood began to flow from her hand where she had caught it on the sharp edge of a brick, but she did not notice it and kept searching for a crack in the wall . . . if she had something with her to set fire to it, perhaps she could burn it ... but there in the old house she had been locked in a silver cage, dappled with flowers, that was the image she had had of herself at sixteen. Burn it? Why did she need to burn it when time had burned it for her? Burned the foolish girl with her foolish smile and her foolish innocence, her lips that waited, trusting, confident, for the happiness that was reflected in her eyes. The wall was nearly at an end and there was no crack. The foolish girl had not thought about cracks in the wall, and why should she? The world was warm and soothing, dazzling as a sunbeam, the world was thrilling as a flash of lightning, genuine as a chunk of pure diamond, a magic carpet that bore her to the peak and set her down there, it urged her on with the joyous peal of silver bells, the colours of the rainbow, with flashes of moonshine on deep, still water, with the song of evergreen, everlasting love ... foolish girl! The wall was solid as a prison wall.

The wall came to an end and there was no crack ... perfection, Mohamed said and, after him, Rafik. Things are relative. That's enough talk of absolutes, the tower is a dove tower and the owner of the house is not strange. Anything short of the Devil can be put up with, Rafik said, everything in this world of ours is possible, anything can happen and there is no better place than this. Every house has an owner and the landlord here may be the lesser evil, it's all a game, that's the best way to describe how you have to behave her mother said and so did her father and everyone else, everyone. Every stage of the game was calculated, here, there, everywhere.

Samiya wondered if what she saw was a glimmer of light, or if she was imagining it. Was she still a foolish girl, at twenty-five? There was a glimmer of light shining out from the threshold of a closed door, of that she was certain, and she had to wait to go through that door.

Samiya went back to the car and stretched out on the back seat to wait. She soon fell into a sleep stronger than her fear of feeling cold, than her hope and her despair. She awoke to the sound of the *muezzin* making the call to prayer, and shrank down where she lay as the door creaked open, making enough noise to wake up the whole street as the landlord came out, the veins standing out blue on his hands as his fingers crushed his prayer beads, his lips twisting as he recited his ritualistic imprecations to God. Once the landlord had gone, Samiya slipped into the house.

She crossed the rush-covered path that led to her new home, knocked gently on the door and stood waiting for a moment, as the watchful, wakeful eyes in the tower drilled into her back. The door opened a crack and Rafik appeared, fully dressed, on the threshold. The cigarette between his lips quivered as he smiled, surprised, and stepped back to let her in. Once he had closed the door he cried:

'Is this your wife, Mohamed? !'

Mohamed came rushing out of the bathroom carrying a sheaf of papers in his hand, and it fell to the floor as he looked, astonished, at Samiya. He seemed remote, distant to Samiya as he stood looking at her like that. Without thinking, she put her hands to her hair to set it straight and they came back smeared with mud. Rafik said, as the smoke from his cigarette gathered and hung in rings on the air:

'What is it, Mohamed, don't you recognize her?'

He leaned his head to one side and gestured with his left hand, still holding the lighted cigarette, as he introduced them to one another:

'Zahiya . . . Mohamed.'

'What happened, Samiya? Why have you done this to yourself? All this time we thought you were sitting in the car. Rafik was just going out to find you.'

Samiya watched the smoke rings stretch out one after the other. She replied in a neutral tone, without a trace of reprimand:

'I was waiting for you to open the door for me.'

Mohamed reached out his arm to Samiya. He

almost touched her waist but then let his arm fall to his side.

'I wanted to, but . . . I beg you to understand the situation, Samiya,' he said.

Mohamed and Rafik exchanged a glance that cast Samiya far away, isolated, outside the circle. For the first time in her life she felt embarrassment in Mohamed's presence and she wished he could not see her as she was, smeared with mud. Rafik crushed his cigarette underfoot on the tiles and said:

'Thank Heavens we're safe. If he hadn't happened to go out, Samiya would have put us through Hell . . . I . . .'

Mohamed gently stopped Rafik from finishing what he had started, his nose wrinkling as he gave a little laugh to break the moment of tension. Samiya looked at his face closely and realized that a long time had passed since she had last seen that face . . . a year and seventeen days. She was startled, as if she had not been aware of time passing until that moment. Mohamed patted Rafik on the back and said:

'Shame on you, old man . . . the girl's putting herself out for us.'

The circle isolates Samiya, excludes her, takes her far away alone, as her eyes cloud over and she concentrates on the clock pendulum that moves back and forth, seeming as if it will almost stop but not quite stopping as she sits on the dentist's chair and the drill gnaws into her mind and turns, touching the nerve and stops, to touch it again. Samiya noticed that the papers which Mohamed had dropped were scattered all over the sitting room, and she found herself on her knees, gathering them up, her hand shaking, only to let them fall again as the pendulum drilled into the nerve. Mohamed leaned over and held her hand. He said:

'It doesn't matter, Samiya . . . go and take a bath and change your clothes.'

She clutched at the papers as they fell, trying to gather them up again as if everything depended on setting them in order. She stood up, sighing, and put the papers on the table, setting them straight as the clock pendulum crawled back and forth. They did not sit straight. Mohamed dragged her over to the bathroom and, before he closed the door behind her, he thrust something into her hand. When she gave him a questioning look, he said:

'A change of clothing,' he said, 'the clothes you're wearing are no good any more.'

Chapter 6

Somewhere between waking and sleeping, Samiya felt a pair of eyes gazing at her and she murmured, pushing the day from her and clung to sleep ... sunbeams were shining like diamonds on the crests of the waves as she struck the wave with her hand, next to Mohamed's hand which vanished into the blue and came out again like a white dove. Her body softened under Mohamed's gaze, flowed with grace and beauty. Where had her beauty come from? Mohamed was looking at her, his eyes shining. He vanished into the water and she waited, quivering, for him to come back and look at her, call her name, pick her out from everyone else and she flowed, delirious, into the water. Mohamed shook the water from his hair and the twisting spray coiled around them both, isolating them from everyone else. He whispered: Do you know what you're like today, my love? You're like a water nymph. Without thinking, she set her swimming costume straight over her full, taut thighs. At that moment, she realized she was beautiful and she laughed. She almost fell in love with herself, with the golden skin of her face, taut as a drumskin, with her little feet which Mohamed warmed with his breath before she went to sleep, with her rounded cheek which sloped smoothly to her ear, as Mohamed said, and with the nape of her neck from which she was forever pushing back her hair.

Samiya came up to a higher level of awareness that dissipated the dream and left her trapped between the black bedposts. Her eyes wandered over the room in surprise . . . Mohamed was sitting at the table with his back to her. There were papers on the table, the cracked mirror, the bench with its insides spilling out, the clock pendulum swinging dully back and forth as she kneeled on the ground, gathering papers that had fallen and would not be set straight. Yes, it had been difficult when she met Mohamed yesterday, with all that disappointment, that sense of exile, crisis, awkwardness. She had not imagined it would be like that. The flood, the unbroken torrent that she had held back had broken yesterday and so it had been difficult. Was it because so much time had passed? But time could not change her love. Our love is stronger than time whether he is with me or not, she said to her mother, reaching into the void to rescue his image, which grew more splendid with every day. Was love everlasting another one of her absolutes? Or was it the world outside that weighed heavy on her, stemming the torrential flood, dictating the apprehensive look in her eye, the poised tension in her lips, her self-absorption, her calculated words and gestures? Was it impossible for love to last for ever here? With the landlord here, he and Rafik – where had Rafik gone? And the eyes in the tower, the torch dazzling her, a knock at the door, or had the time and place for that passed, was it time for the invasion? Who was going to invade? Rafik was not there now, that was for sure.

Samiya wanted to call to Mohamed. She stood up before she did so, picturing him sitting on the pink rug in the sitting-room at home, making space for the guests, his head leaning over to one side as usual, listening attentively to the conversation, listening well and talking well, breaking the ice, making people feel at home, inundating the whole place with his warmth. Suddenly, he raises his eyes to her, shining as he realizes that she realizes, and the gleam in their eyes binds them together as one and, for a moment, cuts them off, separate from everyone else; they exchange a conspiratorial glance as if they had managed to do something others rarely do, and pulled it off in a crowd of people without their realizing it. He leans his head to one side again and listens to the guests. Her pulse races as she sings a victory song to herself over and over again: I'm not alone any more, my love, I have demolished the prison of the body, I am you, my love, I am with you in your veins, in your blood I flow, in the beating of your heart, in the pulse of your thoughts, in the gleam in your eyes, but where has Rafik gone? Had he been with them from the start, from the very start, hostile and invasive? The strange thing was that Mohamed had never made any fuss when Rafik was always visiting. With a little self-confidence he might be a magnificent man, Mohamed said. Rafik is the opposite of me in every way, my opposite, she said, proud of the contrast and when Mohamed said, in another context: There's nothing more like something than its opposite, she did not forgive him.

Samiya looked at Mohamed, sitting hunched over his papers with his back to her. She was astonished, as she always was, by how straight his hair grew at the nape of his neck, in a line straight as if it had been drawn with a ruler, showing up the contrast between the blackness of his hair and the smooth, polished ivory whiteness of his neck. Mohamed offers sweets to the guests in the sitting-room, stands in front of her, laughs for no reason and stuffs the box of sweets into her lap, touching her hand without thinking. From the touch, she knows and he knows and the wave sweeps over them again. After a little while we will get rid of this crowd and lock the door, after a little while. He laughs and she laughs, for no reason, he busies himself and she busies herself, both feeling that they must put themselves out for their guests as if they owed them an apology, as if they wished to make up to them for something they had missed without even knowing it. They carry on, chatting to this one, charming that one . . . after a little while, as they insist with the most sacred oaths that it is still early, laughing louder than they had done before the evening drew on late into the night . . . after a little while, nothing is sweeter than waiting. Mohamed looks at her, his eyes shining, and people say how beautiful she is, how good and kind and, finally, she closes the door behind them, filled with love for them, those poor people. Samiya rolled over and whispered, her voice tender:

'Mohamed.'

Mohamed, surprised by the sound of her voice, turned sharply to look behind him and, seeing the empty look in his eyes, she sat bolt upright. Gathering up his papers and carefully setting their edges straight, he gave her a welcoming smile and said:

'Hello, Samiya. I didn't want to wake you, I thought I'd leave you to get some rest.'

She looked at him, watching him as he spoke. There was something strange in the tone of his voice, in the expression on his face, in his movements. What had changed? Was polite restraint putting boundaries between them, or was she imagining it? There was something old and something new in his tone, his expression, his movements. What did it remind her of? He sat on the end of the bed and said:

'So did you sleep well?'

Samiya pressed her legs together with her arms and said, lightly:

'Fine, thanks.'

'I've missed you a lot, Samiya,' Mohamed said and she replied:

'I've missed you too,' realizing that she felt awkward and confused. If she had not, she would have been able to express the depth of her feelings more eloquently, especially now that she almost had him back, after all the exile, all the turmoil . . . I am you, my love, I am with you, I have demolished the prison of the body, in your veins with your blood I flow . . . but where has the gleam in your eyes gone? Did he feel awkward and confused as well?

Samiya looked at Mohamed as he sat on the end of the bed, his legs together and his hands intertwined, and wondered where the torrential flood that had united them had gone. There was something old and something new in the way he was sitting, in his tone, in his expression and in his face that said: Let everyone set his own boundaries. Her lips trembled ... Samiya, declare your love to Mohamed, Maha said, even just hint at it. Impossible, she replied, when I see Mohamed all wrapped up in himself like that do you know how it seems to me, Maha? He seems like a smooth, round speck of quicksilver which you think you have a hold of but which slips out between your fingers. Just like a silkworm in its cocoon, Maha laughed. Their life together could not come to an end as if it had never been, their relationship could not go back to point zero, the beginning of the beginning.

Samiya touched Mohamed's nose with her fingertip. He held her hand and she pulled it away and, confused, set it on the palm of his hand as his fingers ran over her and his forehead creased in what looked like a frown ... his forehead creased as he thrust a carnation into her hand and turned his back on her at one of the parties they had gone to at the beginning to see each other, parties they had left together just like anyone else. Samiya pulled her hand from Mohamed's and, without thinking, put it up to set her hair straight.

'I think I look wrong,' she said and to point zero she returned. How could she say so, when everything in this world of ours is possible, anything can happen, said Rafik. Mohamed was straining his ears.

'Do you think someone's coming?' he asked, breathing a sigh of relief as she did when the footsteps drew away.

'What were you saying, Samiya?' he asked and she muttered, awkwardly, in reply:

'Nothing.'

Yesterday her breath had hung on the clock pendulum as it swung dully back and forth when Mohamed had said to Rafik:

'Shame on you, old man, the girl's putting herself out for us.'

With the same expression on his face he said: Let everyone set his own boundaries. She had thought she had forgotten that expression on his face, but it had been on his face yesterday, when he stood by the car door and asked: What about you, and again at dawn when he said: I beg you to understand the situation, and it was on his face now, when she was going back to point zero. I am you, my love and, if not, tell me Who am I?

Samiya suddenly fell upon Mohamed and

hung around his neck. She felt his face turn from hers for an instant, his body stiffen against her, and she buried her head in his chest. He held her in his arms, stroking her hair with his lips, then he lifted her face to him and kissed her on the mouth with infinite gentleness. Samiya let him kiss her, one small kiss after the other, her lips dry. She buried her head in his chest again, and Mohamed whispered:

'What is it, Samiya, my love . . . you aren't your natural self at all.'

Samiya got up and stood by the cracked mirror as Mohamed stood behind her and took her in his arms again:

'Don't be afraid, my love, don't be afraid.'

Her eyes filled with tears . . . language stood between them again like a wall. The time when he had been able to complete a sentence that she had started had gone. Mohamad went back to the beginning of the beginning when he said:

'I'm sorry I've put you in this position, Samiya.'

For months and months they had turned in an empty circle, both of them knew it, and she had punished him with the reproachful look in her eyes. How long would the silence last? His voice stayed caught in his throat, and both of them passed as strangers among strangers. I don't mind, Maha, she said, I'm still safe and sound, he still hasn't asked and I'm not going to ask about him either. In the beginning, she had been able to say the word 'I', she had been independent of him. But what was she now? I am you, my love, and the circle is complete . . . Who am I? she asked, and she almost heard Mohamed say now what he had said in the beginning:

'I'm sorry, it seems we aren't on the same path.'

Samiya moved his arm from her waist and went over to the bench to sit down. On her way there, she caught sight of her face in the cracked mirror and, without thinking, turned away. Then she turned, slowly to face her image, asking: Who am I? The mirror showed her a lump of flesh with four eyes, a face lost in the darkness, and the question pressed into her mind again: Who am I? Hide me, mother, I am nothing, in darkness shroud me . . .

'No! It can't be!' she cried out.

The light went on in the room and Rafik said, closing the door behind him:

'What can't be?'

He threw a bundle of daily newspapers on to the table and carried a paper bag full of food into the kitchen.

Chapter 7

The circle closed in. Mohamed's picture appeared in the newspapers, with in-depth articles on the story of his escape from prison, as Rafik successfully carried out the tasks he had been set. He hid the car and thwarted the police by telling a number of colleagues about the plan to arrest them. When Mohamed called him his guardian angel, Rafik seemed to have reached the height of his victory and Samiya recalled, as she read the newspaper, how annoyed she used to be as a child by the two angels, one on the right and one on the left, night and day, reckoning people's good and evil deeds. In one of the articles, Mohamed was a Frankenstein and, in another, he was a Marlon Brando plunging the dagger into his enemy's breast, an enchanting smile playing on his lips. Everything is possible, anything can happen in this world of ours, anything short of the Devil can be put up with, the question Who am I? presses into my mind and Rafik is the opposite of me.

Samiya stopped at the third article, in which Mohamed was a schizophrenic, one moment a normal man and the next a ferocious beast, like Dr Jekyll and Mr Hyde, the question Who am I? pressing into her mind. Rafik was delirious, rising to the peak beyond which there is no peak as he confronted the police, his sweat flowing yellow like the sweat of the dead and the crucial moment came when Mohamed said, after four years:

'I'm sorry, it seems we aren't on the same path.'

To point zero she returned, it's all relative and everything is possible in this world of ours, anything can happen. In the fourth article, entitled 'The Man in Hiding', Mohamed was transformed into a chameleon whose colour changed wherever it went. Rafik puffed up at every word of praise from Mohamed and deflated like a punctured balloon at any criticism of what he had done, a look that quickens and a look that kills, a baby's swaddling clothes in two black eyes and a dead man's shroud. According to the article, Mohamed had a tremendous capacity for disguise and could change, even as the colour of his eyes changed and shifted; he had chosen green because it was his favourite colour. Who am I? she wondered and to point zero she returned, the cracked mirror showed her a lump of flesh. Hide me, mother, hide me, I have had enough of trying, in darkness shroud me, Rafik is the opposite of me in everything, my opposite, she kept saying, the light of the torch shining in her eyes as her body writhes without feeling desire, as if that contrast gave her an identity and definition of her own. One of the articles on Mohamed appeared beneath the picture of a singer, who was showing her cleavage to the photographer, with the caption 'Seduction Sleeps: God Curse He Who Wakes Her!' It's all a game, that's the best way to describe how you have to behave, but was that in the old house or everywhere? What if I can't? The question had not arisen when the path that she and Mohamed had followed had forked in two, the event of the escape had been a dangerous first, a thrilling first that posed a challenge to security and order and gave bold heart to whoever still needed encouragement. Rafik said to Mohamed as they sat around the table:

'I swear, I gave the police the runaround — they didn't know if they were coming or going.'

The author of the article reminded his readers

that he had warned the government, in an earlier number of the newspaper, on such and such a date and such and such a page, of the danger of tipping the scales of Justice, but the government had not paid heed nor had Rafik ceased to vaunt himself. The author of the article thanked God for making him able to see the future and prophesy to the blind government, which did not make use of this supernatural ability of his, finishing off the article with question marks, exclamation marks and a series of dots . . . to point zero she returns as the circle closes, what, why does she not find an answer, a baby's swaddling clothes in two black eyes and a dead man's shroud as the question Who am I? presses into her mind without an answer. It was she who created the love that is stronger than time, the love that seemed absolute, and worshipped it.

Samiya's eyes settled on Rafik as he sat with Mohamed at the table, talking. She decided that the opposite of something was the thing most like it: Rafik barges in with his aggression and she slips through with her charm, a look that quickens and a look that kills. Mohamed, really, did not need either one of them.

Samiya started to read again and stopped at the lines that read 'Moreover, the District Attorney's office has found evidence that sheds light on the event, evidence that had been withheld in the interests of the investigation.'

She sat up straight and heard the insides of the metal bench groan as they hit the floor. The circle was closing, there was no time. She had to hurry, to start, to reach – reach what? The woman on her knees, covered in mud, setting straight papers that would not be set straight? The handful of air, the empty look in Mohamed's eyes, the furrow on his brow and I hope you understand the position? What limp stuff was she made of? Could she not stand on her own two feet like everyone else did? Did she love Mohamed as an equal, or love being lost in the other and losing her self? Would she be able some day to bring back by love what she had lost in love . . . be able to move of her own free will, act, take care of herself and be self-sufficient? Mohamed was not innocent of optimism, was convinced that everyone possesses a treasure they are bound to discover and, when that happens, that they will find strength they had not known before. The circle was closing, there was no time. The landlord was there, he and Rafik, watchful, wakeful eyes in the tower, the handful of air and Mohamed was thrusting something into her hand as she stood on the threshold of the bathroom, she did not know what it was, the clothes that she was wearing were no longer any good at all, did she have the power to change? I am the bride, she said, could she some day be content and self-sufficient, and

make the owner of the house play her game?
Lord, grant me the strength to pull myself
together, Samiya muttered, Lord, do not put me
to the test before I pull myself together, and
Rafik said, leaning on the back of the chair:

'Me? The Devil himself doesn't know me. Do
you know me? Who am I? Where do I come
from?' Laughing as he swung on the chair, he
added: 'Even I don't know who I am.'

Samiya stared at him . . . You too? Rafik Fayek
Samih Mahmoud Hussein as much as I am
Zahiya, the bride, clutching at a handful of air?
Are you also a nothing? Did the mirror show
you a misshapen lump of flesh, a face lost in the
darkness? What would you do if you were put
to the test and the mirror no longer reflected
your image? Samiya found herself suddenly
sitting up straight as Rafik picked up the newspaper, pointing to the lines that had caught her
eye. She watched Rafik read out loud as a whis-
tling sound rang in her ears . . . You too? God
help you, the day they demand the truth from
you, the truth of you as you are, the day you
face yourself and ask Who am I? into the trap
she falls, Who am I? Mohamed asked, sounding
a little annoyed:

'What is it?'

Rafik replied:

'What are they talking about? This is such a
cliché.'

Mohamed smoothed out the newspaper and folded it. Casting an anxious glance at Samiya, he said:

'By the way, we have to be ready for any eventuality.'

Rafik dismissed all that was in the newspaper with a wave of the hand, and Mohamed patted him on the shoulder, insisting that they had to stay alert. Samiya looked at Rafik. His face had come alive again. You too? God help you, the day you are no longer waiting for anything, when you can't be sure of anything, in the trap where the mirrors are blind and do not reflect your image to you, delirious, and where the walls are deaf and do not echo your voice to you, victorious. Rafik said to Mohamed:

'The only important thing begins with the attack, he springs without waiting, goes to where the danger is and clings to it, every part of him taut, swoops once, wipes out with a single blow all that lies before him and like an eagle flies.'

Samiya's lips trembled . . . God help you when the path is blocked and you can't mount fear and say the word 'I', when you are not waiting for anything, when the mirrors are blind and the walls deaf, in the trap where you wander, vacantly, asking Who am I? God help you and God help me, the circle has closed.

Chapter 8

'Do you still love me, Mohamed?' Samiya asked apprehensively, sitting on the end of the bed with Mohamed standing at her side. He laughed, dispelling her misgivings and said, sitting down next to her and hugging her:

'Is that the sort of question you should ask? Of course I love you, Samiya . . . do you doubt it?'

She turned her face away, and he whispered:

'There are plenty of things to worry about here, Samiya, please don't worry about something else you don't have to.'

Samiya protested, running her fingers over his cheek:

'But you've changed completely, Mohamed.'

'It's natural, you have too.'

Samiya said, in tones of disbelief:

'Me?'

Mohamed is with me in his absence, she said to her mother, reaching into the void to rescue his image. As the days went by, her mother's voice insisting that she should go back to the old house began to have the effect that it had lacked at first.

Mohamed said:

'Yes, you Samiya. You're shy as if we were just beginning, strange and awkward.' He added: 'It's been a year and more, Samiya, and the position here is difficult too.'

Samiya muttered:

'The landlord and Rafik . . .'

Mohamed continued:

'You can't reckon things that way, Samiya. We have to take the positive side of things into account, getting out of prison, freedom, the ability to act, the fact that we're alive and can start all over again and cope with new situations.'

Samiya decided that she had to begin again. She wondered if time would help her and the position they were in, things are relative and there is no better time in this world of ours, she had to try, she had to reach somewhere even if the position was difficult now.

Samiya reached out a trembling hand to stroke

Mohamed's hair. She had to act quickly, to get to know – know whom? Herself, her husband? She had thought that she knew him so well she could finish off a sentence he had started and anticipate the direction he would take, but had she really known him or had she imagined she knew him? If she had known him, she did not have to begin again. Nothing stays the same. Was life a series of beginnings, of going beyond and beginning again? She had had to begin again before now . . . the lift had almost reached the top and her wish had not come true, perhaps it never would. She said, her face shining: The first time I saw you, do you know what I wanted to do? They were alone together for the first time. The blood rushed to Mohamed's throat and his eyes misted over as he drew her to him and embraced her. She stepped back, laughing, short, broken laughs . . . that was not what she wanted at that precise moment, the third, the fourth floor, only the fifth and last remained . . . she reached out a blind hand and her fingers settled on the tip of his smooth, delicate ear, her body slacked and she leaned back against the wall of the lift with a sigh of relief. Enough? he asked, mockingly, and she nodded happily without speaking. He burst out laughing as they came out of the lift into the restaurant where he had taken her to dinner.

Afterwards, she had come to know his stolen

and reassuring kisses, security, with him she blazed trails of happiness and despair but he never knew that nothing was complete for her the way that it was the moment he mocked her, the moment someone feels someone else getting to know them and, through them, perfecting their knowledge of all existence, the moment she reached out a blind hand her gaze was drawn back to his ear. She walked by his side, knowing him as she had not known him before. People stared at her as she went to the empty table at the end of the restaurant, they stared at her as she sat down and Mohamed said that day it was because she was beautiful. Neither of them realized that she had stopped time that night and had held the moment in her eyes, the moment of pure happiness and infinite knowledge. She sat down, unaware, not realizing that the moment would soon end and would never be repeated in the same way, the moment the newborn child cries out as he meets life for the first time.

Samiya reminded Mohamed of that moment and her heart pounded as she saw emptiness in his eyes for an instant ... please, my love, do not leave me, do not scatter me like a handful of ashes, stay in my being. I am who I am because you know me and if not, tell me Who am I? A name, a body without a soul, without depth, without roots? She reached out a trembling hand to touch his arm, her eyes hanging on his, beseechingly: I'm not a foolish girl any longer, my love, now I know that life is a mill that crushes the most beautiful part of it, a sieve that sifts out all that is delicate and fine and leaves only the grit. Did I lose myself? It was the first day we were alone together you and I, for months we had been turning in an empty circle, both of us knowing, my eyes looking out for yours and making you suffer: how long would the silence last? Was it our destiny always to flounder around in circles of silence?

The memory was reflected in Mohamed's eyes, a faceless spectre. He struggled painfully with waves of forgetfulness as she began to fill out the features, her eyes flooded with tears. She leaned over to kiss his hand and her body slackened, her exile ended when Mohamed leaned over and raised her face to him with infinite tenderness and their eyes met . . . the past was not in vain, my love, my roots are in the ground, soon I will know you as I never knew you before, I will know myself as never before, soon you will lean over me, your mouth over my eyes, you will start with the left eye and then the right, my eyelids will not mistake the touch of your lips, nor my arms the trembling of your hand nor my breast the beat of your heart, soon, soon we will become that unique creature that is us . . . my isolation will soon be broken . . . Mohamed's body stiffened and

Samiya sat up straight, dizzy as if she had been looking down from a giddying height. They heard footsteps on the stairs. Someone knocked at the door and, when there was no reply, went away.

Samiya stretched out alongside Mohamed in the bed . . . there was no time to get to know someone else, no time for things to grow. Perhaps it was Man's destiny to stand with his face to the wall and his back exposed, perhaps that was his natural and only position in this world, a position he simply had to accept. Things were relative, there was no better position in this world of ours, perhaps there was no need here for things to grow, only the need to forget. The other person in her had to drown in oblivion, that other person who had become detached from her, tense, counting the footsteps. Samiya kissed Mohamed and he kissed her back, but something had been broken. She buried her head apologetically in his chest . . I am conscious and I do not feel you . . . my ears are listening and I do not hear you, my eyes are open and I do not see you, where are you, my love? Where am I? No, I can't forget, hold me to you, my love, hold me, drown my consciousness in oblivion, with powerful drugs dull me, in labyrinths of loss lead me, I did not want you like this nor did you want me like this . . . for us to love, we have to forget, to become lost . . . ahead of us are only moments of loss.

Samiya clung to Mohamed in a frenzy, her eyes clouded over and bulged, her lips twisted and her handsome face lost its looks as she sank into a fit of hysteria. Mad with despair she tried to continue loving and mad with despair he tried. She did not love him at that moment, nor did he love her. Each was using the other to forget, to become lost. Samiya leapt up as the landlord pounded at the door . . . there was no time, not even for loss.

Mohamed whispered to Samiya as she straightened her dress and smoothed down her hair:

'Don't worry, Rafik is coming.'

And he slipped into the kitchen to hide.

Chapter 9

When she opened the door, she found the landlord standing next to Rafik. Sighing with relief,
she stepped back to let them in. The fact that
Rafik was there was a godsend, for it meant
that her role was over. But was it to end, would
she be given the chance to stand on her own
two feet?

The landlord caught up with Samiya as she
sat down, limply, on the bench. Hiding a bundle
behind his back, he said:

'Guess what I have with me?'

Samiya kept a poker face, not to let it be seen
how much she hated him . . . there was an old
feud between them, between her and that man.

But who did he remind her of, what did he remind her of? All she was certain of was that it was an old feud and that things would not be finished until she had settled it with him. The landlord said again, enjoying the game:

'Guess what I have with me?'

Samiya found herself playing his game and wondering when she could make him play her game, by the rules that she laid down.

'I don't know, you win,' she said, as she had heard Rafik saying to Mohamed in the car: Bravo . . . your wife is a real *maestro*. The landlord seemed a little annoyed that Samiya had ended the game so soon. But she knew the rules of the game and she did not give him the chance to protest, so he turned around to carry it on with Rafik – who answered, tersely, that it was time to go to sleep and so, without meaning to, opened the gates of Hell. The landlord leapt up into the air in a gale of laughter, his *galabiyya* flapping open like a hot-air balloon.

'You don't sleep . . . and neither do I,' he said.

Nervously, Rafik asked the landlord what he had seen and he replied, with perfect clarity:

'I see you. All day and all night, I see you.'

A faceless, animal fear swept over Samiya, making her certain that it would always be with her, draining her until she settled her old feud with the owner of the house. Rafik moved to nudge him in the ribs, but let his arm fall heavily back to his side. He pulled over a chair from the table and straddled it, hugging the back of the chair. Samiya was afraid he would burst into tears. But instead, he said:

'You win.' Then he sat up straight and began to rock the chair back and forth, looking at the landlord and muttering:

'Tsk . . . tut . . is that the way for a landlord to behave?'

Samiya wanted to leave everything behind and run away. The situation had become impossible: the landlord had found out that Mohamed was hiding there, so what was all this tortured charade for, now that the question of what to do had become completely irrelevant? God help you and me . . . the circle had closed. Rafik was still intoning in the same, choked voice:

'Tsk . . . tut . . . is that the way for a landlord to behave?'

The landlord rubbed his eyes with his finger-tips, as if he were about to cry. Rafik swooped down on him and said, angrily:

'What did you see?'

'It's my house and I'll do as I like in it,' the landlord said, in that rich, deep voice of his that did not fit with his frail body. He added, with a note of finality: 'I'd like to make that perfectly clear.'

'What did you see?' Samiya asked the landlord in a honeyed voice, hoping to conceal her sense of misgiving that had almost become a certainty. Her interruption lifted the moment of tension, fraught with danger, between Rafik and the landlord who was now ready to carry on with the game. Shrugging his shoulders, he said: What is it to me anyway, and then buried his face in his hands to show that he was embarrassed by what he had seen. Rafik leaned over and nudged him in the ribs, asking in honeyed tones what he had seen. The landlord began to jump up and down, his *galabiyya* ballooning open in the breeze chanting:

'I saw . . . I saw . . .'

Rafik played along with him, leaning forward and then sitting up straight each time the landlord spoke and, each time, asking:

'What?!'

The landlord stopped, beckoning Rafik and Samiya to come close so that he could let them into the secret. Samiya tried to stand up and found that, weighed down by the faceless animal fear, her body had turned to jelly and so she sat down again. The landlord ignored Rafik's attempts to monopolize his attention, insisting that Samiya come close too. Rafik, losing his patience, dragged Samiya over, shouting: Put us out of our misery! and almost falling to the ground as Samiya leaned on him with all her weight. Trying to recover his balance, he shouted at her, asking what was going on as she leaned on him like a child learning to walk. She leaned her back against the table. Rafik's voice was choked with tears as she chanted, like a child playing:

'Here she is . . . here she is.'

The landlord scampered between them and set the bundle that he had been hiding behind his back on the table, behind Samiya. Placing one hand on Samiya's shoulder and the other on Rafik's shoulder, he said, briefly:

'I saw everything.' He grimaced, pulling his head down between his shoulders until it almost disappeared. Then he pointed at both of them and said:

'You and he don't . . .'

Samiya turned her back on him and leaned both arms on the table. Rafik was forced to stay silent this time, and the landlord continued:

'You and he don't sleep.'

Rafik's hand tightened on the back of the chair as if he were just about to lift it up and break the landlord's head open with it. Instead, he sank into the chair, facing the kitchen, turning his back on the landlord and on Samiya. The landlord went up to Samiya as she leaned, her arms bent, over the table. As she leaned back to avoid him, he leaned back too, almost sticking to her. She leaned to the right and he leaned over to speak to her. She realized that this time the game was more than she could cope with and she wanted to run away, far away but she was paralysed by that faceless, indistinct animal fear.

The landlord crouched down on his knees, looking at the table through Samiya's arms. His face lit up, and he sat up on his knees. He reached out his hand until he was almost touching Samiya's right arm, then pulled it away and, suddenly, thrust his hand between her waist and her arm, snatched the bundle that he had left on the table and ran towards the kitchen where Mohamed was hiding.

Without thinking, Samiya found herself leaping up behind the landlord. She grabbed the tail of his *galabiyya* and held on until he fell to the ground.

A loud explosion rang out as the landlord fell. Fragments of glass scattered around the room and, before she fainted, Samiya heard the landlord wail:

'The bulb . . . the kitchen bulb has blown.'

Chapter 10

Once she had come round, Samiya decided that fainting was her way of escaping from a situation that she could not bear. She found herself stretched out on the bed, with Mohamed sitting at the end of the bed and Rafik sitting on the bench, smoking, a frown on his face. The landlord was not there. Was he really not there, or was she possessed by him as he swathed her in that faceless animal fear that vanquished her and made her want only to run away? Samiya wanted to know what had happened after she had fainted, and whether she had aroused the landlord's suspicions when she had pulled him to the ground.

'Of course you messed everything up, and without any call for it,' Rafik replied, before Mohamed could stop him. He advised Samiya to rest and try to get some sleep, and she was content knowing that everything had turned out all right. She insisted on clarifying Rafik's comment that there had been no call for what she had done, and Mohamed told her that there had been no call for her to be so on edge as he had not been in the kitchen when the landlord had gone in there. How? Samiya asked, sitting up. Mohamed told her that he had predicted the moment of danger and had jumped out of the kitchen window into the garden and closed the shutter. He had climbed back in once the landlord had left, as he and Rafik had planned. The last detail gave Samiya pause for thought. Why am I here? she wondered. Feeling like slapping Mohamed and Rafik, she stretched out on the bed and turned her back on them both . . . what danger those two could have averted from her, what danger! The blood drained from her legs and arms as a harbinger of death, or at least paralysis. If she had known beforehand that Mohamed had somewhere to hide when he needed it, she would have been able to cope, she would have dealt with the landlord calmly like anyone else. If she had known, she would not have pulled him to the ground and made him angry and suspicious, she would not have fainted. Everything here was planned, prepared, carried out at a distance from her. Everything here was completely remote from her, so what was making her stay in this place? Why were they deliberately keeping things from her? Was it out of pity, or out of contempt, or because they believed that if she knew what was going on she would be able to spoil everything? From the moment the journey had started, she had shared nothing with them except, of course, the fear – and she had not even shared that with them. Not knowing what was happening made her more afraid, led her to do all kinds of insane things that made it all the more dangerous, rather than less risky. Had it happened because she knew nothing, or because she was unable to stand on her own two feet? Her wild outburst on the stairs at home expecting that Mohamed had been released when he had not, her wild rush from this place to fetch Mohamed back from the car, and the landlord with his beer and 'the night is young', a night in the open – it was pure chance, Rafik said, that you didn't spoil everything. Her being here was a hindrance rather than a help, so what was making her stay?

Samiya sat on the bed to eat. Under the insistent gaze of Mohamed and Rafik, she tried to concentrate on her hand as she raised the food to her mouth and put it down again, as little pieces of boiled egg went down into her stomach as if she had swallowed the whole egg, as four eyes stared at her in silence and the clock pendulum swung dully back and forth, breaking the silence that settled over the room. Samiya set the tray of food aside without finishing it.

She came out of the bathroom after she had washed and dressed. She stood, hesitantly, in the sitting-room for a moment and Mohamed suggested to her that she rest. She slipped under the covers without saying a thing, as her mother asked her as she usually did on the telephone: What are you waiting for alone? And she, which she did not usually do, muttered: Nothing, nothing at all, pulling the white sheet over her head. Samiya felt her eyes burning like hot coals in their sockets as the train repeated: It's over, it's over, and she knew that she would only cry at the end of the journey. When she reaches the old house, she will cast herself down in the stairwell and weep, the cries of the women in black whipping the sound of her weeping into a shriek. Samiya mumbled in her sleep, wondering why the women in the old house were always in mourning. Mohamed asked:

'Are you sleeping, Samiya?'

She began to feel weighed down by the fact that Mohamed and Rafik were there. She listened carefully. Perhaps they were talking. A heavy silence hung over the room, laden with accusations that made the air throb, accusations on the point of taking shape that did not take shape. Samiya rolled over, turning her back on Mohamed and Rafik, and their eyes, full of condemnation, followed her in silence, branding her. If either one of them would speak she would know the nature of her crime, would at least be able to make out what it was that she had done . . . was it that she had weakened, failed, loved Mohamed, married him, or that she had ever been born? But neither one of them spoke, and nothing broke the silence but the ticking of the clock pendulum, swinging back and forth, back and forth like drops of water melting away stone, and the sound of a match striking against the box whenever Rafik lit a cigarette. Anything would have been easier to bear than this silence. Was it her destiny always to be beating against walls of silence? She had to pretend that she was asleep, now, right now. Samiya shuddered as she imagined what she would hear if she pretended she had fallen asleep. Rafik no doubt would start off. He would look at Mohamed and say:

'What's with you, what's with this marriage? The strange thing is that everyone warned you, old man. She'll be a burden on you all your life.'

Mohamed would reply:

'I had thought that one day she'd be able to stand on her own two feet.'

Rafik would come back:

'The dead don't stand on their own two feet.'

No, Rafik would not say that. Rafik lacked imagination, and he would only be aware of that fact when he had gone through something comparable and not before. Perhaps Mohamed might say that, but he was something of an optimist and, according to him, a person only dies when his heart stops beating. Mohamed would sit back and pronounce his familiar wisdom: Everyone has a treasure inside and if you look deep within yourself at the right moment you will find it, even if you never dreamed it was there before. Open Sesame, and the door opened up on to Mohamed's treasure. Would it ever open up on to hers, and when? How little this man knew, how little he understood. Samiya pictured Mohamed sitting down, relaxed as always, his eyes, tender as the eyes of a poet, bright with the inextinguishable flame that seemed to burn deep within him and his lips, firm as the lips of a prize-fighter, lit by the same fire. She pictured him sitting, at peace with himself, content, complete, not needing anyone else. What did she mean to him? Indeed, what did Rafik mean to a man who was content with himself, a man with inexhaustible resources? Samiya hated that integrated wholeness about Mohamed which she once imagined she had managed to break through . . . if he had been weak, what heights could she have risen to if he had needed her to? What heights had he kept her from, that man, with those brilliant eyes and radiant lips? If he had wept on her breast, she would have hidden his head in the night of her hair, she would have stopped herself from breathing for fear that it might disturb him. But he did not weaken, he claimed that he understood and gave her that look which drove her crazy, a knowing look without knowledge, perceptive without perception. The strong do not understand the weak. Rafik understood her better than Mohamed did. Rafik was closer to her than he was, a look that quickens and a look that kills, a baby's swaddling clothes in two black eyes and a dead man's shroud, as the earth underfoot gives way without reason, gives way. She had not failed to do anything. She had done all it was possible to do and all that was impossible too, she had squeezed herself out to the last drop so that not even the dregs remained. Rafik continued:

'I know that sort of woman, she's like a leech who wants to suck a man's blood until she's done with him.'

Samiya shook with rage as if Rafik had actually uttered these words. She leap up and rushed over to draw back the inside bolt of the door. Mohamed leapt up after her and Rafik cried out a warning. Samiya pressed her face against the door.

'I'm going to choke in here,' she said. As Mohamed patted her on the shoulder she added, a weary note creeping into her voice:

'There's so much smoke in the room too.'

Rafik opened the window and said:

'Let's see, where is all this leading to?'

His words were like a starting shot. Samiya turned around, feverish and panting, to face him.

'Yes, that's right say it, curse me and say what you've been wanting to all day.'

'Here we go. Get ready, Mohamed, we're getting into a right bout of hysteria,' Rafik said uneasily. Mohamed went up to Samiya and put his arm around her, trying to calm her down. He realized that she was on the point of exploding and that, if she did and if the landlord heard, it could destroy them all. Samiya pulled violently away from Mohamed and turned to face him.

'You too. Why aren't you saying anything, or have you been killed by your own kindness?'

'Give her a slap, Mohamed,' Rafik said, 'a slap's the only thing that will do her any good.'

Samiya's voice rose, the words rushing out with her breath.

'Say you don't love me, Mohamed, say I'm a burden on you and it was a mistake for us to get married.'

Mohamed said in an admonishing tone:

'Your voice, Samiya. Please control yourself a little, for my sake,' and Rafik said again:

'A slap, Mohamed, give her a slap.'

As she slipped from consciousness, Samiya raved, her words broken by hysterical laughter:

'I thought I gave you what nobody else could give anyone and all the time you didn't want it, could live without it, say that I'm a burden on you, a leech that sucks your blood.'

Rafik said:

'You'll bring the walls down around us soon, you're shouting so loud.'

Mohamed buried Samiya's head in his chest and she escaped from him again and, breathless, stared at Rafik as if she had forgotten he was there. She took a few steps up to him, her face shining with wild joy.

'A bloodsucking leech, a leech. Just like you, Rafik!'

She put her hand to her belly to still the laughter that had come upon her, laughter which turned to howling, a drawn-out howl . . . Rafik lifted his hand, Mohamed cried out, and Rafik landed a slap on Samiya's cheek. A confused look came into her eyes as the blood drained from her face for a moment and then turned red, as she touched the place where he had slapped her. Mohamed pulled Rafik, who seemed appalled, away. He buried Samiya's face in his chest and there was silence for a moment. Then Samiya raised her face, stained with tears, and calmly, proudly said to Mohamed:

'I want to go home.'

She realized at that moment that, for the first time since she had met Mohamed, she was expressing a wish that was not his wish, her very own, particular wish. Mohamed said, realizing that the decision was final:

'Tomorrow morning.'

Chapter 11

Rafik tried to complicate things, seeming as if he wanted to cling on to Samiya. If she left, it would arouse the landlord's suspicions and, if his suspicions were aroused, all would be lost. He could not go out and leave Mohamed on his own, as the landlord might come in while he was out, and he could not stay locked up with Mohamed, as he had more important things to do outside. He was not a woman yet. Rafik grew almost hysterical, saying over and over again that he had to keep moving, do something, swoop, attack, and he would rather die than wait, weak and paralysed, especially in that cramped, stifling little place.

Mohamed smoothed things over, as always, it's so easy for him to smooth things over. The landlord would not suspect anything; they would say that Samiya's mother was ill in the village and she had gone to help her, her mother may be ill for a while, and the risk of the landlord coming to the house would have been a risk whether she was there or not. They had been aware of that when they had put on the padlock outside. Rafik would not be locked up in the house – there was no need, he would just lock the door behind him and when he came back from outside he would look out for the signal they had agreed on and would stay back if he saw from the street that the shutter of the kitchen window was ajar. It was a temporary situation and the two of them could always take refuge with friends while they were finding a new place and making a new plan. It would not be ideal, but things were not ideal as they were either.

Samiya gave a sigh of relief once the question of her going back was settled, and she paid not the slightest attention to Mohamed's final gesture, nor to Rafik's contemptuous look. From the moment she had expressed her own wish to leave, she had turned inward to embrace her fear. Nothing outside touched her or reached her and, like a pregnant woman completely in the grip of the creature growing and stretching inside her, she withdrew, feeling her fear in hidden whispers, footsteps, coarse laughter, seeing her fear in watchful, wakeful eyes that shine like pearls on earth and in heaven, inside and outside the house, set in her heart. Samiya gave a sigh of relief as she realized that the situation would not last. In the stairwell of the old house she would close her eyes and fade away. Mohamed said:

'I think we'd better go to sleep, then. It's nearly dawn.'

He received no reply from Samiya or from Rafik, who had stretched out on the bench and turned over to sleep facing the back of it. Mohamed asked Samiya to come to bed and she gently took his arms from her. He leaned towards her where she sat on the table and lifted her face to kiss her eyes, first the left eye and then the right, then his lips settled on hers. Samiya abandoned herself to his kiss, her lips dry. He looked at her sadly then turned away and went over to the bed.

He fell asleep as soon as his head touched the pillow. Rafik mumbled in his sleep for a while and, when he could not get comfortable, turned over and lay on his back, stretching out his legs along the back of the bench. He took out his lighter and, when it let him down, threw it to the floor. He reached for the box of matches on the edge of the table and lit his cigarette.

There was a long silence as smoke rings gathered and vanished. Rafik whispered:

'Samiya. I'm sorry about what happened yesterday.'

Samiya realized that he was referring to the slap he had given her the day before and she found herself saying:

'It had to happen.'

He gave her a questioning look and she said:

'Somebody had to wake me up.'

'Are you awake?'

Without thinking, she replied:

'I've decided I'm not up to this game.'

No sooner had she said it than she realized that Rafik would say that playing games in this world of ours was a matter of necessity not of choice and that she had to accept things the way they were and if she did not she would keep banging her head against the wall until she died. She accepted that death might be a way of escaping from an impossible situation. Rafik said:

'So you withdraw.'

'I withdraw,' Samiya said, as she realized how frightening the finality of her withdrawal was. Was it a partial or a total withdrawal, she wondered, and was it from this place or from the whole world? The question frightened her, even though it seemed necessary to withdraw at that time. The fear mounted inside her as she hid in the old house, swathed, draped in layer upon layer of dampness that kept her safe, made her fade away. Hide me, mother, hide me, I have given up trying. She kept silent as Rafik said:

'Isn't it a bit early to take that decision?'

He threw his cigarette to the ground and realized that it was still alight. He sat up straight and crushed it out with his foot. For no reason, he crushed it out again, then brought his leg heavily back to its place. He contemplated the fingernail on his middle finger for a while, then raised his head and whispered, urgently:

'Don't go back to the old house, Samiya.'

Samiya gave a weak smile. She would have liked to tell Rafik that it was a long road, and that she was no longer able to carry on down it. She found herself saying:

'It's no use, Rafik. You'll have to go back too.'

'Me go back? Go back where?'

'You'll go back to wherever you came from,' she said, adding with certainty, 'if not today then tomorrow,' not knowing where her certainty came from. Rafik said:

'There's no way I'm going back, Samiya . . . there's no turning back now. I've grown up, Samiya, and I don't want to die in my mother's lap.'

Samiya said nothing. She wondered whether what had happened had really made him more mature, or whether he was imagining it? Rafik broke the moment's silence. He said:

'Do you know how I want to die, Samiya?'

She looked at him, her heart pounding.

'Wounded in the street,' he said, 'then I'd crawl to the highest place I could find and look up to heaven and die.'

He seemed to be longing for this moment of death. Samiya was unable to hide a smile and a gentle look that she had not seen before came over Rafik's face. He said:

'What about you, Samiya? How would you like to die?'

Samiya's smile left her face as she said:

'I'd like the earth to swallow me up, without my feeling, or anyone else feeling that I'm dying.'

Mohamed had woken and was sitting on the end of the bed. He said sarcastically:

'If you don't mind, could we play another game?'

Rafik turned red and gave a forced laugh. Samiya looked out of the window and said:

'It's morning already.'

She stood up to get ready to go out. She passed by the cracked mirror and stopped for a moment to look at the twisted image that looked back at her. This is me, she said, the fear in her eyes wrestling with curiosity, this is me, she said, revulsion wrestling with the attraction in her eyes. She stepped up close to the mirror and reached out her hand to touch her image, to get to know it and, with a weak smile, she stretched out her arms to take hold of the edges of the mirror and embrace it, beads of sweat standing out on her face as her eyes clouded over with a pain close on ecstasy. Samiya turned and went towards the bathroom, her head held high, lost in her own world.

The water damped down the heat of her face as she thrust her head under the tap. She switched it off once she had wet her hair, and chanted: I have failed, drops of water falling from her loose hair into the basin as she kept chanting: I have failed . . . Samiya wrung the water from her hair into the basin and stood up. She drew her hair back and sighed with relief, realizing that she had failed and feeling almost delirious as she got dressed to leave.

Rafik leaned against the front door and his eyes, fixed on Samiya, betrayed the mocking smile that had come back to his lips. Mohamed sat pretending to read some papers. Samiya piled her hair up on top of her head and reached over to the table for some hairpins. Mohamed said, awkwardly, afraid to look at her:

'I think you can catch the eight o'clock train, can't you, Samiya?'

Samiya dug the hairpins violently into her hair one after the other, almost enjoying the pain it gave her each time. She turned to look for her coat and found it over the back of the chair with her handbag and the small suitcase next to it. As she put her arm into her coat, Mohamed picked up her handbag and thrust ten pounds into it.

'You'll need some money,' he said.

Samiya shook her head in protest. The handbag lay on the table between them as they stood facing one another without looking at each other. Suddenly, Samiya snatched up her bag and took out the ten pounds, scrabbling through the bag and scattering banknotes in chaos over the table and, finally, she tipped out all the coins that were in her purse. She took ten pounds and a few coins and then stood up straight. Rafik said as he came towards her:

'Pick up your money, Samiya.'

Samiya looked at Mohamed, asking him to stand by her, knowing that they needed money more urgently than she did. Mohamed was afraid to look at her. Rafik came up to the table and said, his voice choked with anger:

'You'd better pick up your money. If you don't I'll burn it.'

Mohamed said, heaping up the banknotes on the table:

'There's no need to make such a fuss over nothing, Rafik.'

Rafik stepped back. He smiled bitterly and said:

'Samiya has solved her problem. Fine, she'll go home and close her eyes and go to sleep. She's paid the price and she'll go out of that door with a clear conscience. She's paid the price and you've accepted it, Mohamed ... you've accepted it.'

Mohamed put his hand on Samiya's hand before she could give back the money. Her face turned red and she said:

'I ... I don't mean it like that.'

Rafik picked up the banknotes that Mohamed had heaped up and held them up high in his fist, letting them fall back on to the table, one by one, as he laughed mirthlessly. He said, his voice hysterical:

'Well, that's what you've done, Samiya ... Mohamed deserves nothing but these from you.'

Samiya bent down to pick up her handbag and her suitcase. Rafik blocked her way to the door, his voice, caught in a spasm of rage, rising gradually:

'Do you know, the sad thing about people like you, Samiya ... you talk a lot about love and you don't know how to love, you can't give anything ... you're paupers ... paupers.'

'Just like you, Rafik. Just like you,' she replied, unable to continue. Mohamed created a diversion, imitating Rafik's voice:

'A slap, Samiya, give him a slap, a slap's the only thing that will do him any good.'

Rafik shook his head and smiled. Samiya's eyes filled with tears and Mohamed leaned over to kiss her. Putting his arm around her shoulder, he said:

'Goodbye . . . Rafik will take you to catch a taxi.'

Samiya turned down the offer and Mohamed waved goodbye as he went to hide in the kitchen. Rafik followed her outside, saying:

'Make sure you don't forget to drink from the Cup of Cures, Samiya.'

As she ran to the street door, running from the watchful, wakeful eyes, Samiya realized that Rafik could not harm her any longer. She sighed with relief as she slipped out of the door without the landlord stopping her . . . the ritual of rituals . . . the Cup of Cures ritual . . . it only happened when someone came back to the old house seeking refuge, and she would drink for sure from the Cup of Cures, seeking refuge in the Lord of Daybreak from the evil that He created. She had in turn gone back seeking refuge to the house she came from, the house she was going back to . . . that yellow brass cup, engraved with verses from the Qur'an inside and out, an heirloom passed from grandfather to father to son in an endless chain. One after the other they had sought refuge in the Lord of Daybreak and entrenched themselves in the old house against the evil that He created. That thick piece of stone the colour of ivory, cracked and pitted by the years, turns and turns the water in the Cup of Cures. A precious stone, they say. What stone? Where did it come from? Nobody knows and nobody wants to know, the Cup of Cures is best plunged in secrets. The brass spangles fixed by a thread to the edge of the yellow brass cup make a tinkling sound as the thick ivory stone turns and drowns them, all ninety-nine of them, one for every holy name of God.

Samiya pictured the whole scene – she is standing in the middle of a circle of women dressed in black, always in mourning, what had they lost? She does not know. Standing out against the blackness, her grandmother sits on her golden chair that is draped in green velvet, holding the Cup of Cures and muttering verses from the Qur'an, turning the precious stone as the tinkling sound of the spangles hangs amid the total silence that settles over the room. Her grandmother takes the Cup of Cures to her mother, who stirs the liquid again with the precious stone to which the holy names of God gather and then scatter, and then she takes it herself. Her grandmother asks her to drink and, after her grandmother, her mother and then the women in black say, in a sad voice: Drink. She hesitates for a brief moment. She would like to break the circle and leave, and let whoever comes back to the old house drink from the cup seeking refuge in the Lord of Daybreak from the evil He created. Her grandmother says: Drink it down, and then her mother, and then the women in black repeat the words in a sad voice, and she throws back her head and drains the cup to the dregs of the dregs. There is a moment of silence and everyone holds their breath as the tinkling sound fades away, footsteps pass without making a sound as if they had not passed, then the children erupt in a flurry of halleluiahs and rush up to her, run around her, jumping up and down in the air and shouting, they jump higher and shout longer as they dance around the palm cages that they have burned at dawn to celebrate Sham El-Nessim. Her mother hugs her and weeps, why is she weeping? She does not know, and she buries her head, exhausted, in her mother's bosom and weeps too. What is she weeping for? She does not know, but she feels that something final has happened, something that there is no turning back from. It is as if she had taken, as Rafik would say, the fork in the fairy-tale path down the road of no return.

Chapter 12

In half an hour the train will move and, with her eyes full of grit, she will hear the wheels of the train repeating all the way: It's over it's over. No, she will not cry until the end of the journey, in her mother's lap. Hide me, mother, I have given up trying, she will weep . . . I'm in a hurry, she said to the driver who took her to the station, as she tumbled into the front seat of the taxi. The driver asked himself sardonically if she was trying to hurry along death, and grumbled at having such bad luck so early in the morning.

Samiya's eyes settled for an instant on the morning newspapers lying on her lap and she turned her face from them, as the words gathered on the lips of the one-eyed newspaper seller who was knocking on the car window, insisting that she settle up with him. She thought she had given him enough, as the newspapers lay shaking in her lap, but it seemed that she had to pay again. Something was frightening her ... the newspapers and the news they might contain? The words gathering in the mouth of the one-eyed young man ringing an alarm bell? Or perhaps her rash behaviour when she rushed into the middle of the road, making the driver ask himself if she was trying to hurry along death?

Samiya sat down in the carriage and placed the newspapers next to her. Rafik had advised her to drink from the Cup of Cures and had let the banknotes fall on to the table, one by one. An acute sense of duty awoke in Samiya that she had inherited from her grandmother through her mother, a sense of duty that took over their whole lives and made all else worthless. She had to tell herself again that she was no good for anything, that she was a hindrance not a help as she gathered hailstones in a tin plate and her mother, covering her head, shouted at her from behind the window pane: It's no use. Hide me, mother, hide me, I am ashes, I am nothing, I am a monster with four eyes. In darkness drape me, with slumber in oblivion shroud me, I have put an end to my quest, it's no use, no use.

In the darkness I will lie down and I will not

say no, in blackness I will be swathed, in a whisper I will wrap my voice so nobody hears me, I will never raise my voice, with cork I will line my shoes and pass along the winding corridors of the old house as if I were not really there, the corridors will not echo to my footfall. And I will clean my room and clean it again, I will not be content . . . my room is as clean as if nobody were living there, the mirror does not reflect my breath and my pillow does not hold a single hair of my head . . . I will wash my body as if I were washing an ineradicable sin from me and I will wash it again, I will not be done . . . my face shines like a mirror and my hands are pale, I no longer sweat. I wrap the rough towel around my body and scrub myself with it, the last tremor that remains in me trembles and I wrap the towel tighter . . . the towel is not rough enough, the towel is no longer rough. On the table I pile my necklaces, my rings, powders and scents, my costly belongings, my fine belongings, with my hand I touch them, over my cheek I run them, I take shelter in my bed and I dream . . . my belongings have doubled in number, they have grown many and indistinct in the drawers, in the corners of the cupboard, under the bed.

I placed my hand on the bottle top with the pointed teeth and took shelter in my bed, I no longer dream, I dreamed my youth and my middle age and I no longer dream. My head is heavy and my eyes shed tears for no reason. I fastened my hand on the bottle top, no longer feeling anything, in the morning they will find the teeth of the bottle top sunk into my flesh and no trace of blood . . . the dead do not bleed. She died a short, sweet death, the death of the chosen, they will say. They will never know that in the old house died her youth and her middle age.

The sting of the cold from the open train window sent a shiver running through Samiya's body and, for a moment, she felt thankful to be alive.

The station platform was crowded and the train was almost empty. At the last moment they would rush, out of breath, from the end of the platform to throw their bags through the windows as if their lives depended on catching the train . . . the bell rings and the wheels turn and drink, her grandmother would say and after her grandmother her mother and the rest of the women in a sad voice. Something was sounding a warning bell in the newspapers, lying next to her as, one morning, she fled from dead end to dead end and reached the main street without realizing it.

Samiya picked up one of the newspapers and cautiously turned the pages, looking out of the corner of her eye, afraid to read yet wanting to read what was written there. On page seven, she found much more than she had expected . . . a man with a hard face, wearing spectacles and a black overcoat over a white *galabiyya*, came into the carriage followed by a fat woman. The man gave Samiya a searching stare from under his spectacles and she let the newspaper fall to her side. Was he a police informer? Did he know her? It couldn't all fall apart so quickly, so clearly. She must be imagining it, she thought, trying to dispel her fears.

The man turned around to take the cases from the porter, once he had decided to stay in the carriage. He put them up on the luggage rack. The fat woman sat down facing Samiya, turning over a piece of gum in her mouth. Samiya turned over the edge of the newspaper where it lay next to her, mechanically counting the pages and, when she reached page seven, she opened it a crack, afraid that someone would notice her and see Mohamed's photograph next to Rafik's. All my defences have been destroyed, so what am I doing now?

The man brushed the dust from his hands and sat down, once he had finished putting up the suitcases. Samiya looked at his face, stony as a statue, and lowered her eyes . . . I saw nothing, I do not know. If she attracted his attention, Mohamed's colleagues would say as they gathered in the far corners of the factories, on the stone benches and in the porticoes of the universities ... they would lower their eyes out of shame, for she was one of them and she had destroyed him ... I don't know, believe me, I do not know, in my mother's lap I did not see and I did not know, in the darkness of the well a person no longer needs to see and know.

* * *

In the seat by the window Samiya saw a peasant woman carrying a little girl, half-dead. She had not noticed her come in, and thought she must have crept into the carriage on tiptoe. The fat woman stopped turning the gum over in her mouth. She said:

'Shame on you, woman, where are you taking that little girl?'

Samiya muttered:

'She's going to bury her.' The peasant woman lifted the child's arm, which had slipped down heavily into her lap, and put it back, not showing if she had heard. Samiya said again:

'She's going to bury her.'

'Ten minutes to go,' the stony-faced man said, addressing nobody in particular, nothing lasts for ever, nothing lasts for ever, there is no time even for loss, what am I doing when it is a matter of life and death and Mohamed is standing, exposed, with Rafik and they have no one to help them but me? A broken feminine laugh comes from the next carriage, and a man's voice saying:

'I'm not responsible for what happens now.'

The rest of the laugh is lost in an invasive burst of water, this is a matter of life and death, she can warn Mohamed and Rafik that they are in danger and get back to take the next train to the old house.

Samiya was certain that if she went, she would not come back. If she chose to go back to that place she would stay there until the end, one way or another, whether the place changed or not, the same place, the same people, things are relative and nothing lasts for ever. One has to begin and begin again, one has to keep going beyond the situation, and the price of Paradise is Hell, with the watchful, wakeful eyes drilling into her back, are they eyes or openings in the dove tower? A knock at the door and her hand shakes as she slides back the bolt on the front door, how many of our fears are real and how many of them imaginary? The landlord's eyes shine like pearls as he calls out: Who is it? from the threshold. I am the bride, she says, and Mohamed stifles his laughter as Rafik introduces Zahiya to him, come on, let's play. How had she missed the comic element in her situation, in the whole situation? If she had learned how to laugh, perhaps she would have been able to go beyond everything, a feminine laugh in the next-door carriage, her body twists without desire and her lips smile without pleasure, was that a moment of defeat or of victory? The landlord's body is taut and his face covered in wrinkles, things are relative, everything is possible, anything can happen in this world of ours and anything short of the Devil can be put up with, as she runs from one dead end to another, reaching the main road without realizing that she has reached it.

Samiya leaped on to the station platform at the last moment, before the train pulled away.

Chapter 13

Samiya decided that she would seek refuge with Mohamed's colleagues once she had got him out of that place, him and Rafik, safe and sound. She was grateful that there was a place she could run to when she needed it, and hopeful that they could begin again, after being in that place. My back is always covered, Mohamed said, people protect me. The world does not begin and end with the owner of the house, things only start and grow in the shade that the wide world gives, you no longer feel isolated and things take on their true proportions. Fear is possible in the big wide world but it doesn't destroy it. Disappointment is possible too, and impermanence, reality's falling short of the ideal, of what you hope for, and new beginnings are inevitable. Had the time finally come for her to stand on her own two feet and be?

Samiya stepped calmly from the taxi at the corner of the main road. She had thought through what was going to happen next, taking into consideration that the landlord might have found out from the morning papers and the possibility that he had not, and the possibility of her getting Mohamed and Rafik out quietly as well as the possibility that she might have to use force with the landlord. The only thing that would stop her was if the police had actually arrested Mohamed and Rafik, and she dismissed this as the least likely possibility. Everything was quiet in the street with the big iron door in the middle . . . there was no curious crowd outside, no guard, nothing at all. When Samiya pushed the door and it did not move, she was convinced that the landlord was inside and that she had come at the right moment, before he had had enough time to inform the police that Mohamed and Rafik were there.

Holding her breath, she knocked at the door. When she heard the landlord's voice saying 'Who is it?' she let out her breath all at once and kept knocking at the door without replying, knocking harder and harder as she realized that she was longing to meet the owner of the house alone, face to face, to finally make everything clear. Make what clear? She did not know, but she was certain that she had lived all her life waiting for this moment, when they would meet. The landlord was having trouble with the bolt. Samiya leaned against the door, her body quaking with the desire to stand on the narrow ledge that is not wide enough to stand on, to look out from the fourth floor on to the inner courtyard of the school.

She slipped through the door before he could close it in her face, stifling a scream before it could form, as the door swung between the landlord, who already knew how heavy it was, and Samiya, who did not know how heavy it was until the moment she was forced to push death from her on one side of the door.

She pushed her way inside, sending him reeling back from the door as the newspaper fell from his hands, a spray of mud hitting Mohamed's picture and the one of Rafik next to it. She wanted to call out to them but he recovered his balance and Samiya forgot all about Mohamed and Rafik. All that she was aware of now was that the owner of the house was there and so was she, oblivious to all else . . . was this why she had come back?

Samiya realized that there was still time. She leaned over to draw the inner bolt closed, keeping one eye on the landlord. She saw herself advancing on him, moved by ineluctable forces. She tried to stop the madwoman but could not and she advanced on the owner of the house, her eyes staring into his. There was a shapeless, baseless, crazed animal terror in his eyes, faceless fears, and as she advanced on him his eyes were filled with spectres and ghouls and the two angels, one on the left and one on the right, who reckon our evil deeds and her mother's gesture that it's no use, and wrong and retribution and hellfire, the look in her dying father's eyes, ignorance, supplication, nothingness, a look that quickens and a look that kills, destruction, unjust rules, hidden rumours and whispers, a knock at the door, the light of a torch shining in her eyes, footsteps that fall as if they owned the earth and everything on it. The madwoman advanced on the owner of the house as if possessed by a demon and, when she seized hold of him, she realized that she had to kill him or die.

Samiya thought she must stop this madwoman who had become detached from her before she lost her head and finished what she had really come to do. She wanted to ask Mohamed and Rafik to help. The landlord's mouth opened in a scream that did not come out as the other woman smothered him and, with a rapid, snatching movement, fell on him and sank her fingers like claws into his neck. Samiya opened her mouth to call Mohamed but the other woman stifled the voice in her throat: Not yet, you haven't done what you came to do yet. You always wanted to kill him, even before you knew him you wanted to kill him, at school on the ledge that is not wide enough to stand on you wanted to kill him. Not yet, you haven't done what you came to do, nobody but you can settle your old feud with the owner of the house, nobody but you.

The landlord recovered from his astonishment and began to work free from Samiya's grip. She felt the same wave of nausea as when she was forced to confront some kind of violence or ugliness. The landlord sank his teeth into her hands which pressed on his neck, but the other woman did not pause at the pain and sank her claws into his neck ... as if all her life they had never clipped her claws, had not driven the deadly spear into her, had not all her life turned her into a doll with cheeks that the breeze could wound.

The landlord suddenly kicked back with his left leg and caught Samiya in the belly with the tip of his shoe. She fell to her knees in the mud, her eyes watching for his next move, her mind a flame that turned from red to blue and then burned pure as her body tensed. She relaxed a little, then thrashed out in her frenzy, crying: Father, mother, grandmother, minaret that looks over our old house, everyone, yes, I am alive, despite you I am alive.

131

The landlord was riveted in his place and Samiya was riveted in hers, watching him . . . yes, I am she, this is my reality, that you have erased. Violence does not scare me, nor does ugliness, violence is of me and ugliness, because I am alive. After today, I will not wrap the rope of manners around my neck, the rope that erases my being and respect, the rope of the look that quickens and the look that kills, the rope of escape and nothingness, the rope of death. I will not die thirsty because I am embarrassed at having to jostle for water. Samiya pretended to want to stand up and the landlord raised his leg to kick her. She caught hold of his leg and he fell on his back. She fell face downwards by his side, her hands twining around his neck. He asked, anxiously:

'What are you going to do?'

Samiya looked at him and said simply:

'I'm going to kill you.'

The landlord beat the ground in a childish rage and said:

'I didn't tell the police, I didn't do anything.'

His eyes became two watery pearls. Samiya wondered if the obscurity around the landlord was in her imagination, until he said:

'Someone's knocking at the door.'

Samiya listened There was no knocking at the door, and she realized that nobody but the landlord could give them away now. She dug him in the ribs and said:

'Not me, son, play another one,' and laughed until the tears streamed from her eyes. The land-lord said:

'They've come, they'll put you in chains . . . and a rope around your neck.'

Samiya tightened her grip on his neck and, inviting him to join in the game which was *her* game this time, she said with childish glee:

'They aren't coming.'

'They are.'

They threw the words back and forth like a ball until the landlord said:

'They'll put you in prison.'

'Once I've killed you nobody will be able to imprison me,' she replied with calm finality, and she wondered if what she had come to accomplish required her to actually kill him, or to kill him inside herself? It seemed to her that she had killed him. The landlord asked her if she was mad, and Samiya shrugged her shoulders and smiled. Perhaps she was mad, that was what Mohamed and Rafik would think. They would never know that she had really come back to kill the owner of the house. Samiya leaned over him and asked:

'Who are you?'

The landlord looked at her, his eyes cold. She asked him:

'Where do you come from? How old are you?'

He threw a handful of dust into her eyes and she doubled over, wiping the blindness from her eyes. He kicked her over and over again as the darkness turned into light. Samiya stayed curled up on the ground without moving, playing dead once she had regained her sight until the kicking stopped. As soon as the landlord turned around to run to the front door, Samiya leapt up behind him and grabbed him by the legs. The old man's head hit the front door as he fell to the ground, and a muffled ringing shook the air. As the blood flowed from the wound in the old man's forehead, Samiya realized that everything was possible in this world of ours, anything could happen.

She cradled the old man's head in her lap. The wound seemed no more than a light scratch. She pulled the ribbon from her hair with a heavy hand and wiped the wound with the end of it. The old man opened his eyes and she wrapped the ribbon under his chin and tied it over the top of his head to stem the blood.

Flocks of doves flew from the tower that had seemed so terrifying before. There was still hope for a new start. Holding the tired old man's head in her lap she called out to Mohamed and Rafik, whose picture looked out from the morning paper where it lay on the ground.

DATE DUE